i'm Not Sam

i'm Not Sam

Jack Ketchum
Lucky McKee

CEMETERY DANCE PUBLICATIONS

Baltimore
❖ 2012 ❖

Cemetery Dance Publications
132-B Industry Lane, Unit #7
Forest Hill, MD 21050
http://www.cemeterydance.com

The characters and events in this book are fictitious.
Any similarity to real persons, living or dead,
is coincidental and not intended by the author.

ISBN-13: 978-1-58767-353-5

Cover Artwork Copyright © 2012 by William Neal McPheeters
Cover Design Copyright © 2012 by Desert Isle Design
Interior Design by Kate Freeman Design

I'd like to thank Paula White, Alice Martell and Kristy Baptist on this one—they each know why, perfectly well—also Carolyn, Ana, and Jaimie at the bar, for their little-girl dress-up tips.
—Jack Ketchum

There are two names on the cover of this book, but no one would see those two names together if it weren't for a third: Alice Martell. Thank you, Alice, for representing our work with Class. I think we make a fine trio, and here's to more. Glad to be Your Client.
—Lucky McKee.

From Lucky McKee:

"The nicest thing in the world you can do for anybody is let them help you."
—John Steinbeck, SWEET THURSDAY

From Jack Ketchum:

"Love is friendship caught on fire."
—Bruce Lee

introduction

by Jack Ketchum

IN EVERYDAY LIFE THERE ARE NO STARTS OR STOPS. Even the most startling, life-altering events— unless they're fatal—are buffered and buffeted by other events, constant and ongoing, so that the impact of any one of them is muted.

Not so in fiction. Fiction's like music. It starts and stops in silence. First there's no music and then there is and then it's gone. And again like music—if it's any good—that silence at the end should have a bit of resonance beyond itself. A loud or quiet buzzing in your ear that satisfies both you the reader and that particular story.

Because fiction wants to make a point. Sometimes many points. It wants to make you stop and think and feel at the end. So it needs its clear delineations, its exclamation points, its opening and closing curtain. Life has only one closing curtain. And it sucks.

I'M NOT SAM STARTED OUT ITS LIFE AS THE IDEA FOR a short story which Lucky and I planned to adapt into a short film.

Then the damn thing started growing.

The root premise, which was a simple one, kept sprouting new shoots and branches and leaves as we worked it through in our daily Instant Mail messages to one another. We got a little crazy. We fell in love with the characters. We had fun.

Pretty soon though, as we started writing the prose version, it became clear that what we had on our hands was going to be novella-length, not a short story—and a fairly long novella at that. No problem. A novella's just about a perfect length to adapt into a feature anyway. With a short story you have to expand and add on. With a novel you've got to compress and subtract.

The thing is, the rules and exigencies of prose are not the same as they are for film. Prose is a whole lot looser.

THE MODERN FILM, MOST OF THE TIME, IS DIVIDED into three clear acts. This—as a lot of writers and directors will readily tell you—is a pain-in-the -ass case of the tail wagging the dog. Because the acts are defined not by complexity of story or the director's vision but by simple running-time. Distributors and movie houses want to turn their feature over every two hours or so to maximize showings, hence draw in the bucks. The days of *Spartacus* and *Ben-Hur* and magnificent overtures and slowly drawn curtains are over, folks.

The first act of a movie today is probably twenty to thirty minutes long. It sets the premise, introduces the characters and kicks off the action. The second is probably forty-five minutes to an hour. It complicates the situations suggested by the premise and enriches the characters. It tries to pull you in deep. Then along comes the third act. The third act hopefully ties up all the loose ends set in motion thus far, brings things to a head, makes you glad you've plunked down your hard-earned money instead of sitting home with a beer watching cable. It's again about twenty to thirty minutes in length.

There are no such rules for prose. Sure, there's a beginning, middle and an end in any prose worth reading or writing *but there's nobody standing over your shoulder with a stopwatch while you're doing it.* The beginning can be a couple of paragraphs long if you want. The end can be a single punch to the gut.

So long as you adhere to the rule of silence.

A silence that has resonance and meaning.

WHEN WE FINISHED *I'M NOT SAM* WE FELT WE'D played our music pretty well. We were happy and satisfied with the piece. We felt it worked.

That it worked *as a novella.* But not as a movie. Not quite.

The end, in fact, *was* a single punch to the gut. Perfectly okay as far as we as prose-writers were concerned.

But as a film, it lacked a third act.

Bummer.

Lucky and I work pretty well together, though. So it didn't take us long to agree on a solution.

Sam would remain as she was, a stand-alone novella. We weren't going to try to expand her. But we'd go on to write another piece, a direct follow-up to the story, picking right up where *Sam* left off—a story which would have a different kind of resonance altogether—called *Who's Lily?* So that's what we did.

As a film, the two would run seamlessly together. But here, on the page, each would stand alone. Same characters, wholly different themes and tones.

So here's where you come in.

WE'D LIKE TO ASK YOU A FAVOR, LUCKY AND I. Hopefully you won't find it too pushy of us to be doing so. We're only asking because we think it might add to your experience of the thing, make it more fun for you and more fun for us thinking that you might just indulge us on this one.

If you like what you read in *I'm Not Sam*, there could easily be a temptation to dive right into *Who's Lily?* immediately. As though it were simply another chapter in an ongoing tale. One blending into the other. Almost as though it were life, and not fiction. We'd like to ask you not to think of it that way.

We'd like to ask you to slow down. Take in the starts and stops.

To let *Sam* settle in a while.

A few minutes. A couple of hours. Maybe a day. Whatever.

We'd like to ask you to listen a while to the silence of the first tale before you draw open the curtain on the second. They're playing quite separate tunes, I promise you.

Feel free to tell us to go to hell.

It's your dime. You have every right.

But we're trying to make a little music here, you know?

Couldn't hurt to listen.

—April 27, 2012

i'm Not Sam

IWAKE UP IN THE MORNING TO ZOEY'S CRYING.
I've heard it before, many times. It's familiar.
It's not the usual sounds cats make, it's miles from
a *meeow*. It's more of a muted wail. As though she's
hurting. Though I know she's not.

It sounds as though her heart is breaking.

I know what it is.

She's got that toy again.

Zoey's a tuxedo and so is her old stuffed toy. I don't
recall who gave it to her now, some friend of ours
who likes cats I guess, but that was long, long ago—
and though there's a tiny patch of stuffing leaking
out over the back of its left ear, it's miraculously still
intact, after years between my twenty-year-old cat's
not-always-so-tender jaws.

She protects that toy. She gentles it.

And there's that yowl again.

I glance over at Sam beside me and see that she's
awake too. She yawns.

"Again?" she says and smiles.

Zoey pre-dates Sam in my life by nearly nine years but she loves this cat as much as I do.

"Again," I tell her.

I get up and shuffle across the chilly hardwood floor and there's Zoey out in the hall looking at me with those big golden eyes, her toy face-up lying at her feet.

I lean down to stroke her and she raises her head to meet my hand. I use this opportunity, this distraction, to steal the toy with my free hand and tuck it back into the waistband of my pajamas.

I pet her head, her long bony back. She's arthritic as hell so I'm very gentle with her. I know exactly how to touch her, the exact weight and pressure of my hands on her body that she likes.

I've always been able to do this. With animals and with people. I've always known how to touch.

And here comes the purr. Soft these days. When she was young you could hear it from rooms away.

"Hi, girl. Good morning, good girl. Hungry? Want some foodie?"

Yes, *foodie.*

Cats respond to an *i-e* sound. Damned if I know why, they just do.

She trots ahead of me into the kitchen, a little wobbly on her feet but always game for breakfast.

I pull her toy out of my waistband and give it a good toss into the living room. She'll find it sooner or later but for now there are other things on her mind.

That toy. That tuxedo with roughly her own markings. There's a mystery to that little stuffed animal. One I know I'll never penetrate.

It's the only toy she ever cries over. All the rest are passing fancies. She bats them around awhile and then loses interest. I find them gathering dust beneath the sofa, in a corner under my desk in the study and once, on the grate in the fireplace. How it got beyond the screen only Zoey knows.

Zoey came scratching at my door one cold March Saturday evening. She wanted in. I was drawing in the study when I heard her. I opened the door and there was this scrawny cat, probably six months old at the time the vet said, with mites in both ears, a sweet disposition, and obviously starving.

I always wondered where she came from.

We're pretty much out in the middle of nowhere here.

She came to me spayed. So she had people somewhere. Somebody had cared for her.

Were there others out there? I wondered. Her mother, maybe? Was she part of a litter?

And at some point I started to ask myself, could there be a connection between toy and cat? Could this small inanimate object possibly remind her of something? Family? Was that maybe why this ordinary, no-catnip stuffed tuxedo kitten seemed to resonate for her, to stir something long and deep inside? It seemed possible to me. It still does.

If you heard the *yearning* in this sound she makes, you'd understand why.

It was years ago I got to considering that. I remember feeling at the time that I'd stepped into mystery, into the realm of the inexplicable. Into enigma.

I've never shaken it. It gets me to this day, every time.

IN THE KITCHEN I PICK UP HER WATER AND FOOD bowls and put them in the sink and while she sits waiting patiently I open up a can of Friskies tuna and egg and flake it into another, fresh bowl, pour her fresh water and put them on the floor and watch her set-to.

I hear water running in the bathroom. Sam's up. I hope she gets out of there fast. I've got to pee. By the time I've got the coffee brewing she's standing behind me with her hand on my shoulder and we're both of us staring out the window over the sink out onto the river.

It's a lovely spring morning. Hardly a breath of wind in the trees. There's a bald eagle gliding thermals over the water. He hits its surface and veers away toward the pastureland beyond the far bank and he's made a catch. We can see the gold glint of fish scales in the sun.

Hardly a day goes by when you don't see some sort of wildlife out here. We've got foxes, coyotes, wild pigs. Zoey stays inside. She'd never have made it to twenty if she didn't.

I turn around, give Sam a peck on the cheek and head for the bathroom. She smells like sleep and fresh soap.

On Sam, not bad at all.

I'm not much for breakfast—just a coffee and cigarette kind of guy. I figure food can wait on my break from the drafting table. But Sam is. The coffee's ready and she's already poured herself a cup with cream and sugar and I can smell the raisin bread in the toaster.

I pour a cup for myself and sit down at the big oak table. I like my table. Found it at an estate auction in Joplin. Hell, I like my entire house. We're surrounded by five dense acres of woods and a river, like a surprise waiting to happen.

The living room is all stained wood with high oak hand-carved beams maybe a hundred years old. There's an ancient stone fireplace. The room opens to the kitchen so I'm looking out at all this space in front of me.

It occurs to me—watching my wife of eight years slather her toast with butter and strawberry jam— that we've made love in practically every square inch of it. All over that hardwood floor. Couch and overstuffed chair.

Scorched her lovely ass one night on the fireplace. The memory of which makes me smile.

"What?" she says and swallows her toast.

"I was just thinking."

She squints at me. "You've got that look, Patrick."

"Do I?"

"You do. And what I've got to do is finish my breakfast and pee, shower and drive forty-five minutes to Tulsa so I can autopsy Stephen Bachmann and decide whether it was pills, scotch, plain old Dutch stupidity or any combination of the three that put him in our drawer. I don't have time for you."

"Awww…."

"Don't 'awww…' me, mister."

"Awww…"

"How's Samantha coming?"

"She's about to blow her brains out with a shotgun at the behest of her tormenters. By tomorrow I should have her resurrected. Tomorrow or Saturday."

She takes a long, man-sized swig of coffee, gulps it down and smiles.

"I'm still not sure whether to be flattered or distrustful of the fact that she's named after me. You splatter her brains all over the wall for godsakes."

"Yes, but then she comes back. And I would never splatter you."

I love it when she arches her right eyebrow that way. She gets up and steps over, leans over and kisses me. It lingers.

After all these years, it lingers.

She breaks it off.

"I know, I know," I tell her. "Shower, pee, brush your teeth and off to your Dutchman. You want company? In the shower I mean. Not the Dutchman."

"I don't think so. Maybe tonight, after work. I'll reek as usual. What are we doing for dinner?"

"Leftover teriyaki-beef bourguignon. From night before last. You liked it."

"It was yummy," she says and disappears around the corner into the bedroom.

I hear her Honda Accord pull out of the driveway a half hour later and think how lucky I am. I'm doing what I want to do, drawing my graphic novels—and making a pretty decent living at it. I've got a home I love, a well-loved old cat, and this forensic pathologist person who's crazy enough to love me.

I'd say I go to work but that would be a lie. I go play.

Play goes well.

When I hear the Honda pull back in again, the bloodsplatter pattern on the wall behind Samantha's head is complete. I'll have Sam check it for accuracy but I've learned a lot from her already and I think I've got it right.

Splash page indeed.

It's nearly seven o'clock, getting on to dusk, her normal arrival time. I've fed the cat and the bourguignon is simmering on low. The garlic bread's buttered and seasoned and awaiting the caress of the broiler. All I've got to do is boil the broad-noodles, pour the wine and dinner's ready.

I cover the work, get up and stretch and pad barefoot into the living room just as she's coming through the front door. I realize I haven't put on a pair of shoes all day. One of the perks of the game.

I walk over and hug her and plant one on her cheek. She really doesn't reek. She's already showered at work. She always does. But sometimes, with the really bad ones, it's a three-or-four-shower evening. Tonight, just a little tang of something in her hair. Just enough to let me wrinkle my nose at her.

"I know," she says. "It wasn't the Dutchman."

"No? What did the guy in?"

"Booze, a Pontiac and a obstinate oak tree. He had a nice dinner before he died, though. Saurbraten, red cabbage, potato pancakes and about a pint of vanilla raspberry-twirl ice cream. But the scent you detect belongs to somebody else."

"Who?"

"Gentleman named Jennings. Turkey-farmer."

"Ah, that lovely ammonia smell."

"Right. He had all this turkey-shit piled up next to his barn. Looks like he was about to spread it out over his field when he had a heart attack instead. Fell right into the stuff. He was covered with it. We figure he was breathing in it for a good half-hour before he died too. The inside of him almost smelled worse than the outside. Did you say something about a shower this morning?"

"I did."

"If you wash my hair you're on."

"I love to wash your hair."

"You hungry yet?"

"Not really."

"Turn off the stove."

SHE TURNS THE SHOWER ON, LETTING IT WARM UP and I watch her undress. As always she's businesslike about it but to me she's a Vegas stripper. At thirty-eight she looks twenty-eight, everything tight, the bones delicate. We've both felt sad from time to time that she's infertile, that we won't be having any children. Me a bit more than her I think—I've got a brother for what he's worth and a father and mother while she's an only and both her parents are dead. So maybe I'm more used to family. But I shudder to think how far south her body might have gone were that not the case. It's shallow of me I guess but as she is right now, she's a joy to behold.

She throws the curtain and steps into the tub into the spray of water and I'm right behind her, watching her nipples pucker, watching her glisten. She turns toward me and shuts her eyes. Her long hair's plastered to her head. I reach for the Aussie Mega and lather her up.

She smiles and makes these little *mmmmm* sounds as my fingers dig in for a good, firm, gentle massage. Little lava-eddies of shampoo roll over her collarbone, over her breasts and down to her navel.

"I think I could go to sleep like this," she says.

"Standing up?"

"Cows do it."

"You are no cow."

She smiles and tilts her head back to rinse, straightens up and wipes the water from her eyes. Then looks down at me.

"Oh," she says. "Oh, really? Already?"

"I guess so. Turn around, I'll do your back."

She does. I wash her back, her ass, her breasts, her stomach. She raises her arms and I wash her armpits, her arms, then her back and ass again, into the crack of her ass, into her cunt. She soaps her own hand and reaches down to me.

She's got my cock in her hand stroking the shaft and rolling around the glans and my fingers are moving inside her, my other hand clutching her breast and we're both of us making sounds now. She's gone baritone.

I know exactly how to touch her. I know exactly what she likes.

And god knows she knows me. What she doesn't know is that my legs are giving out and I'm coming all over her ass.

"Okay, enough!" I tell her. She gives me this look over her shoulder. "For me I mean."

"Thank *god*," she says. And she comes too, for the first time that night.

THE SECOND TIME SHE COMES WE'VE ALREADY closed my own deal and I've got three fingers inside her. There's debate about whether the g-spot really exists but she's living proof there's *something* there. She likes this hard, not smooth and easy like in the shower so that's what I'm giving her. She's starting to buck and groan and I'm grinning down at her like I'm listening to my favorite rock 'n roll song of all time.

Then she says those magic words.

I'mmmm commming!

I could cry or laugh out loud, this is such fun. I stay with her, ratcheting up the pace, the pad of my thumb buffing her clit, fingers pressing hard, sliding along the warm wet wall of her insides.

Oh! she says and *ohhhh!* and holds the moment suspended inside her so I hold too while she trembles all around me and then lets go. I work her a little more, smooth and gentle now and she jerks and spasms. Internal electricity. I know the feeling.

She laughs. The bawdy laugh. The one reserved just for me.

"Bastard!"

"You love it. You know you do."

"I know I do."

She kisses me the way you kiss your lover when he's made your day. I kiss her back. She's made mine.

WHILE I'M HEATING UP THE BOURGUIGNON, preheating the broiler for the garlic bread and boiling water for the noodles I ask her to go into the study and have a look at Samantha, see if I've got the spatter right. She comes back in a little while.

"You've been doing your homework," she says. "Studying the photos. Good."

We've got morgue photos and crime-scene photos pretty much all over the place. In my study, in the bedroom, on the bookshelf in the living room. We have to hide them from the guests.

I'd made the mistake a few years back before her mother died of leaving a series of full-color shots of a Mexican drug dealer lying by the roadside—his severed arms and legs piled on top of his chest and his head split open by a machete—left it on my drafting table when her mom flew in from Boston. One look and her face went white.

Try explaining to a sixty-five-year-old woman that this was research for what she'd consider a comic book.

"It's pretty much perfect," Sam says, "in a larger-than-life kind of way."

That makes me feel good. She's got it exactly.

"Right. That's what we're after. Realistic and over-the-top, both at once."

"I can't wait to see how you're going to put her back together."

"Neither can I."

Dinner's fine. I don't burn the garlic bread and the noodles are *al dente*. We're lingering over our second glasses of Merlot when I get this *look*.

"What?" I ask her.

She smiles.

"I was just thinking," she says.

UNUSUAL FOR ME TO GO TWICE IN ONE NIGHT but not unheard of and we've had that excellent dinner and the wine. There's a familiar moment of unease when I glance over her shoulder at the glassed-in hutch and her eight, thirty-year-old Barbie dolls are staring at me, not to mention Teddy Davis, her very first teddy bear, threadbare and crunch-nosed, with these strange, droopy, deeply-cleft buttons for eyes— buttons that actually *resemble* slanted squinty eyes— and this down-turned pouty mouth, so that he looks sort of like Bette Davis on heroin. It's unnerving.

But that passes. She sees to that.

And this time, for me at least, it's even better.

I go a lot longer and she's right there with me all the time. We're a two-man band. She's on rhythm and I'm on lead. She's figure and I'm ground. We don't exactly come together but it's so damn close that I'm still hard inside her when she does.

We always make love with the light on. We figure the dark is for sissies. So that when I roll away I'm able to see the sheen of sweat down her body from her collarbone to her thighs. Sweat that's part her and part me.

And I think, *don't ever let this stop. Don't ever let us get so old or tired or used to one another that we don't want this.*

The thought comes to me just as I'm about to nod off to sleep.

BE CAREFUL, BROTHER, WHAT YOU WISH FOR.

I WAKE TO A SOUND I'VE NEVER HEARD BEFORE.

It's the middle of the night, it's pitch black but I'm awake so fast and so completely it's as though somebody's slapped me.

It's a high thin keening sound and it's sure not Zoey with her toy. I reach over to Sam's side of the bed. It's empty.

I pull the chain on the bedside lamp and the bedroom suddenly glares at me. That keening sound rises higher and more urgently, as though the light were painful.

I see her. There she is. On the floor in the corner wedged between the wall and the hutch, facing the wall, her naked back to me, her arms clutching her knees tight to her chest. It's not cold but she's trembling. She glances at me fast over her shoulder and then away again but I see that she's crying.

That sound is Sam, crying.

But I've heard Sam crying when her mom died and it doesn't sound anything like that. This doesn't sound like her at all.

I'm up and out of bed, going to her, to take her in my arms and...

"Nooooooo!" she wails. ***"Noooooooo!"***

It stops me dead but I think, that's not her. *That's not her voice.* All the time knowing that's impossible.

"Jesus, Sam…"

"Don't!"

And now her left hand is darting through the air over her head like she's shooing away a sudden flock of birds.

I reach for her. She sees me out of the corner or her eye.

"Don't…touch!"

To me the voice seems maybe an octave higher than it should be. What the *fuck?*

"Don't touch," she says, a little calmer this time. Through sniffles. And that's when it hits me.

It's a little-girl voice. Coming from my Sam.

Under other circumstances I could almost smile at the sound. *Sam playing the widdle durl.* But these are not other circumstances. The look in her eyes when she glances at me is not funny.

Okay, she won't let me touch her but I need to do something to comfort her. Plus she's naked. For some weird reason that bothers me. I get up and pull the blanket off the bed. Kill two birds with one stone.

I go down on my knees behind her and hold the blanket out to her.

"Sam, here. Let me…"

She bats at me with both hands, hard and fast, and now she's crying again.

"Don't touch me…you *hurt* me!"

"Hurt you? Sam, I'd never…"

"Not Sam!"

"What?"

"I'm not Sam!"

And now I'm way beyond confusion. Now I'm scared. I've slid down the rabbit-hole and what's down there is dark and serious. This is not play-acting or some waking bad dream she's having. She's changed, somehow overnight. I don't know how I know this but I sense it as surely as I sense my own skin. This is not Sam, my Sam, wholly sane and firmly balanced. Capable of tying off an artery as neatly as you'd thread a belt through the loops of your jeans. And now I'm shivering too.

In some fundamental way she's changed.

But damned if I'm simply going to accept it. I put on my best comfort voice. Comfort and reason.

"Of course you are. You're Sam. You're my wife, honey."

"Wife?"

She stares at me a moment, sniffles, wipes some snot from her upper lip, then laughs.

Actually, she giggles.

"Not your wife. How can I be your wife? That's silly."

I wrap the blanket over her shoulders. She lets me. Clutches it close around her.

"I'm Lily," she says.

THERE ARE SILENCES THAT SEEM TO PEEL AWAY LAYER upon layer of brain matter, leaving you as stupid as a gallon-a-day drunk.

"Lily," I say finally. Or at least I think that's me.

She nods.

I get up off my knees and sit on the bed. Our familiar bed.

She's stopped crying. She sniffles but that's all. I'm still getting these distrustful looks, though. I notice Zoey sitting in the doorway, glancing first at me, then at Sam and then back at me again, like she's trying to puzzle out the situation as much as I am.

"Why do you say that? That your name is Lily?"

"Because it is."

I point to Zoey. "Who's that?"

"Zoey," she says.

"And me?"

"You're…" I see tears welling up in her eyes again. "You're…I don't *know* who you are!"

Then she's sobbing. Her whole body heaving.

I can't bear to see this. I don't know what to do but I've got to do something so I get off the bed and go down to her again and before she can stop me I wrap my arms around her. She tries to wriggle free of me at first but I'm nothing if not tenacious so I hold on and her body's betraying her anyway—the sobbing's got hold of her bad.

It takes a while but at last she subsides. Her muscles seem to drift slowly from high-wire tense to slack. I'm stroking her head exactly like you would a little girl's.

She seems exhausted.

"Come on. Let's get you to bed."

I lift her carefully to her feet and point her toward the fourposter.

"No," she says.

"No?"

"No. Not there."

I want to ask her *why not there* but I don't.

Maybe I figure it doesn't matter. Maybe I'm afraid to know the answer.

"Okay, the couch? That all right?"

She nods. She turns and I see her staring into the hutch, frowning.

"What? What's the matter?"

"You locked up Teddy. I want him. I want my Teddy."

Good grief. She wants the goddamn bear.

"No problem."

I throw the latch and open the glass doors, pluck him out from amidst his Barbies and hand him over. She hugs him to her breasts. And I'm about to tell her hang on, I'll just get some sheets and a blanket and pillow when she's already stepping out past the cat and down the hall into the living room. She seems to know exactly where she's going. Zoey follows along behind her.

I gather up the bedclothes and a pair of light pajamas I know she likes and when I get into the living room she's already lying down, holding on to Teddy. Zoey's curled up at her feet.

"I brought you your pajamas. Can I get you anything? Glass of water?"

She shakes her head. Lets the blanket fall away and stands and steps first into the pajama bottoms and then slips into the shirt and buttons it up top to bottom. She's not shy about it. I'm watching her. It's a woman's nude body I'm watching her clothe but the movements are wrong somehow, they're quick and jerky, full of restless energy, without Sam's smooth flow and glide.

Where are you, Sam?

She sits down on the couch. Looks at me. Like she's studying me, trying to figure me.

"I could have the water now," she says.

"Sure."

In the kitchen letting the water run to cold I'm aware of her standing behind me in the doorway. I pour the water, turn off the tap and when I turn around I could almost laugh. She's standing there straight-legged, with her hands on her hips and head cocked to one side. A kid's cross-examination pose.

"Who are you, really?" she says. Then pauses, thinking. "Are you my daddy?"

Her voice is so very small.

"I'm...no, Lily. I'm not. I'm not your daddy."

There. I've said it. I've addressed her by the name she wants me to use. Lily.

"Who then?"

"Patrick. I'm Patrick."

I hand her the water and watch her gulp it down. She hands me back the glass.

"I'm sleepy, Patrick."

"I know. Come on."

I fix the bedclothes and fluff the pillow. There's something I've got to know. I tuck my wife in. My wife who thinks she might be my child. I'm sitting beside her on the couch. She's watching me. Holding Teddy. It takes me a while and she must be wondering what I'm thinking but I finally get up the nerve to ask her.

"Back in the bedroom. You said I hurt you. How did I hurt you?"

She shrugs.

"Come on, Lily. Tell me. How? So I don't do it again, y'know? How did I hurt you?"

She shakes her head.

"Where?"

She gazes down and slowly pulls away the blanket and sheet over her thighs, and points.

Points there.

THE FIRST SCOTCH DOESN'T HELP NOR THE SECOND. No way I can go back to bed. No way I can sleep. So I sit in the dark in our overstuffed chair and watch her, fetal on the couch, her face as innocent as a baby's.

I'm wondering what the morning will bring. Is it possible she'll sleep this off and I'll have my Sam back again? And where in hell did this come from in the first place? The phrase *multiple personality disorder* keeps banging around in my head like a soup spoon on a frying pan.

What's next? A teenage boy who likes to burn things?

I know her history. Her childhood was apparently just fine. Nobody abused her. Not as far as I know. There were no traumatic car accidents. When her father died she was twenty. Nobody in her family got murdered. There were the usual middle-class adulteries in the family but nothing that would scar her.

So where does this come from?

The hour of the wolf arrives and with it that peaceful eerie silence it has, when the night-creatures go to ground just moments before the birds greet the day. The sky out the window slowly brightens. She turns in her sleep. I finish my third scotch. Its magic has eluded me.

I've worked a few things out over the course of the night, though. So that whichever way this goes I know what I've got to do. At least initially. I get up and rinse out my glass in the kitchen and get the coffee going. I sit down at the table and at some point realize that I've been staring at my hands.

Are these guilty hands?

Don't touch! You hurt me!

This stings. This aches.

And then I think, no. That was a woman I was touching. My wife. And she was touching me back. I won't have the fucking guilt. I won't permit it. I didn't hurt her. I knew exactly how to touch her. She came for godsakes. Three times.

The coffee's down. The buzzer buzzes, telling me so.

I stand at the table and there she is in the doorway, yawning, arms stretched out above her.

This is the moment. Either she'll want the coffee or she won't. I can smell it rich and sweet and so can she.

"Is there juice?" she says.

There's a lump in my throat like something won't go down. These hands are sweating now. But the thing is to maintain control.

"'Morning, Lily."

"'Morning." She thinks for a second. "'Morning, Patrick."

She shuffles over to the refrigerator, opens it, pulls out the grapefruit juice and then hesitates, puts it back on the shelf and takes out a carton of Newman's Own All Natural Virgin Lemonade instead. She turns to me.

"This okay?"

"Sure," I tell her.

BREAKFAST IS COFFEE FOR ME AND RAISIN BRAN with milk and a glass of lemonade for her.

"I've got to make a few phone calls," I tell her. "Why don't you go play with Teddy for a while, okay?"

"Okay. Can I have the dolls too?"

"The Barbies?"

The Barbies are collectors' items by now. I hesitate. She pouts. Hell, they're hers, not mine.

"Why not."

I pull all eight of them off the shelf and arrange them sitting along the edge of the living room table for her. When I leave the room she's smiling.

Back in the kitchen I use the wall phone. I dial her office first. It's early so I get the machine.

"Miriam? Hi, it's Patrick Burke. Listen, Sam won't be in today. Something fluish. I'm calling Doc Richardson. She probably just needs a shot and some antibiotics and she'll be fine. But you'll have to cover for her, okay? Sorry. Thanks, Miriam. Talk to you soon. 'Bye."

Next the good doctor. Who we've known for years.

"Hi, Doc, it's Patrick Burke. I know it's early, but if you could call me back as soon as you get this I'd really appreciate it. Something's up with Sam and I'd like you to see her right away if it's at all possible. I'm kind of… I'm really kind of at my wits' end, Doc. Thanks, Doc. I'd really appreciate it. We're at 918-131-4489."

I repeat the number slowly and hang up. My cheeks are hot and my heart's pounding. It isn't shame or guilt or even anxiety. It's fear. I feel like Doc's my one and only lifeline. What if he has no idea what to do? What then?

I pour myself another cup of coffee. When my hand seems steady enough I take it with me into the living room. Two of the Barbies are undressed—the 20's flapper and the one in the 18th century handmade gown, both of which she designed and created herself—and Sam's busy swapping clothing.

She looks happy.

I sit and watch her for a while. She pretty much ignores me. She's humming something but damned if I know what it is. Sam's not much of a singer but Lily seems to have perfect pitch.

Goddamn.

A half hour later the phone rings.

DOC RICHARDSON SAYS HE'LL SEE US RIGHT AWAY. I've made up the guest room for her—since something tells me she's not going to be wanting to sleep in our bed while she's still this Lily person—so I lay out a pair of jeans, an Elton John teeshirt and a pair of panties on the bed. No need for a bra. She never wears one except for work. But it occurs to me to wonder if, as she is now, she'd even know how to put one of the damn things on.

I tell her to go brush her teeth and get herself dressed. But first she's got to arrange the Barbies and her Teddy *just so* on the bureau across from her bed. I watch in the bathroom while she brushes. It seems to take her forever and she's awkward about it. As though the toothbrush were too big for her. It's very weird.

We're going on a little trip, I tell her. She wants to know where. To visit an old friend, Doc Richardson, I tell her. *Oh*, she says.

"You remember him?"

She shakes her head. Very definite about it. *No*.

She wants to take Teddy along. Fine.

In the car I have to remind her to buckle up and need to help her with the strap. As we're driving she's dancing Teddy around on her lap singing *Frosty the Snowman* in that high clear voice that's suddenly hers even though Christmas is still seven months away.

The doc's office is on the corner of Main and Steuben Street, flanked by Bosch's Hardware and the Sugar Bowl, our local soda shop, on either side. There's a parking spot three cars down from Bosche's so I pull in. She flings open the door, forgets she's buckled in, lurches against the seatbelt.

"Easy," I tell her and press the release. She smiles in a way like *silly me* and flings open the door.

"Uh, leave Teddy, okay?"

She frowns for a moment, but then shrugs and seats him neatly in the passenger side and slams the door. I come around and take her hand.

We look pretty normal, I think. Husband and wife out for a stroll. And Sam, at least, looks happy.

Which is probably why, when Milt Shoemaker exits the hardware store, a bag in each hand, there's a big grin on his face as he walks toward us.

I try to match it.

"Milt."

"Patrick. Miz Burke. Fine day, ain't it?"

"Sure is, Milt."

He's a big man carrying too much weight on him. He's sweating and snorting like a bull.

"Listen, Patrick. I need to apologize to you. I ain't forgotten about those widow-makers you got up there. It's just that with those storms last month I been busy as a two-dollar whore in a mining camp. Pardon, Miz Burke."

I glance at Sam. She's still smiling. Maybe a bit *too* much.

I want to get us gone.

Milt runs Shoemaker's Tree and Stump. It's six months now since he promised to come out to our place with his crane truck and shear some high dead limbs off our old oak tree—struck by lightening last year—about twenty yards from the house. Dead limbs are brittle and dangerous and prone to falling at very inconvenient times. A tourist in New York's Central Park was killed by a widow-maker last year.

I'd wanted his chain-saws out there as soon as possible. But I think, not now.

"No problem, Milt. Tree's held up so far."

"You should call the office and make an appointment, Patrick. That way I'd be sure to get to it pronto."

"Well, I may just do that."

"You should. Out of sight, out of mine, y'know?"

Mine?

"I will, Milt. I will call. You take care, now. Best to Elsie. You have a good day."

He's looking at Sam strangely. A puzzled look.

So I glance at her too.

Good grief. She's picking her nose.

I can't fucking believe it.

"Have a good day…" he mutters as we pass him and walk away.

A DOCTOR'S OFFICE SHOULD HAVE MUSIC, I THINK, to lighten things up a bit. Doc's doesn't. Walking into Doc's is like walking into a sepulchre. The second we close the door behind us I can feel Sam stiffen. I can tell she doesn't like it. There are two old stringy ladies seated whispering in a corner, clutching their handbags as though fearful of a city-style mugging. There's a bald man in suspenders reading a newspaper.

When he turns the page it's the loudest thing in the room.

Thankfully, we know none of them.

We walk past them to the counter. Millie, Doc's receptionist is typing at her desk. She gets up smiling as we cross the floor.

"Hi, Patrick. Hi, Sam."

"Not…"

I cut her off. "How've you been, Millie?"

"Not half bad, Patrick, for a little old lady. You two have a seat. The doctor will be with you in a minute."

I'd outlined what the hell was happening on the phone as best I could and Doc assured me he'd see us right away. I hope he keeps his word. The ladies are eyeing us as we sit. And Sam starts fidgeting immediately.

There are magazines on a low table beside us. I'm tempted but I don't want my own page-turning to add to the din.

Sam's staring straight ahead at the counter. I wonder what's so interesting so I follow her gaze. There's a big three-quart glass jar on the counter and it's filled to the brim with wrapped hard candy—what appear to be cinnamon and grape and peppermints, lemon drops and lifesavers and root-beer barrels.

"Patrick?"

And that little-girl voice coming from this big-girl person gets everyone's attention.

"When we leave, okay?"

She sighs. "Oh, okay."

Millie opens the door. "Mrs. Burke?"

I get up but Sam doesn't recognize her name of course so I lift her gently by the arm and walk her to the door and I see she's confused so I whisper to her that it's all right, she shouldn't worry, and we follow Millie's ample figure to the Doc's office. We enter and she closes the door.

Doc rises, all six feet five inches of him. I clear my throat.

"Doc, this is Lily."

He extends a meaty hand. "Lily," he says, smiling.

Doc's about the warmest, friendliest person I know and if he weren't a giant and had a little more of that snow-white hair on his head and a matching beard he could pass for Santa with the best of them. She takes his hand and shakes it.

"Sit down, Lily. Make yourself at home. Patrick? Can I talk with Lily alone for a little while? Would you mind? Get to know one another a bit?"

There's a small dish of the same hard candy as on the counter in the waiting room sitting on his desk. He pushes it toward her, selects a root-beer barrel for himself and proceeds to unwrap it.

"Help yourself, Lily," he says. He pops it into his mouth.

"Call you in a bit, Patrick," he says around it.

I'm dismissed.

BACK IN THE WAITING ROOM THE LADIES ARE EYEING me with suspicion. I've jumped ahead of them in line, after all. With this strange woman. A story across the clotheslines.

I pick up a copy of *Time* magazine. Astronomers have found a new planet that orbits three stars. There are articles on last year's continental freeze in Europe, on what it means to be a Conservative in America. Britain is banning photoshopped ads in which the models look *too* perfect.

I can't concentrate.

People magazine? *Scientific American? Cosmo's* out of the question with those ladies present.

I solve the problem by doing nothing at all.

And I'm only a bit surprised when I wake up to a hand on my shoulder. Millie's.

Sam's standing beside her. She doesn't look disturbed at all or the least bit unhappy, which is good.

"Ben would like to see you now," she says. "Lily? Here's a magazine."

Sesame Street.

"We won't be long," she says.

Sam settles in with the magazine and I follow Millie inside.

Doc's sitting behind his desk making notes in a folder I can only presume to be Sam's. I sit across from him and he puts down his pen. He shakes his head.

"Patrick, it's the damnedest thing I've ever seen. Physically she's just fine, same old Sam as always. The only physical changes I can see are those she's apparently made by choice, for lack of a better word. The vocal change is all tongue-placement. The jerky movements to the limbs and shoulders, you and I could imitate them pretty easily if we concentrated on it hard enough. So the question is not what she's doing but why she's doing it."

"You mean you think she's faking?"

"Not at all. Quite the opposite. Talking to her just now, there's this strange kind of disconnect. It's as though she remembers selectively. She knows who Lady Gaga is but not her mother's or her father's name."

"She knew Zoey. Our cat."

"Did she now. That's interesting. The only time she got the least bit nervous or upset was when I asked her who you were, who Patrick was. That seemed to confuse her. I didn't push it. But she can identify everything around her perfectly well. I'd point to a chair or a window or a bookshelf and she'd rattle the word for it right off. I knew when she got bored with it too. You could tell. Her vocabulary, by the way, is at about a five-year-old level. She could identify flowers but not the vase, for instance. Called it a jar. She can add and subtract but not multiply or divide.

"This…transformation. What strikes me most is that it's uncannily consistent. Sure, you and I could imitate each of these child-aspects of hers if we tried. But I doubt very much if we could imitate them all at once, choreograph them all together—and do it for hours at a time, as you say she's been doing. That would take one hell of an actor."

He pulls out a prescription pad, picks up the pen and writes.

"Here's what we need to do. First, eliminate anything physical."

"You mean, like a tumor?"

"I've never heard of a tumor causing these kinds of symptoms but yes, a brain-scan's definitely in order.

I want you to phone this number at Baptist Regional and arrange for it right away. I'll call ahead and grease the skids for you as soon as you're out of here, tell them to slip you in ASAP, tomorrow if possible."

He tears off the paper and hands it to me.

"Go home and make the call. Then try to get some sleep. You look like hell, Patrick."

I get up and head for the door. He's right. I'm suddenly exhausted. But one other thing's bothering me bigtime.

"Doc, what if this isn't physical?"

"Yeah, I know. Multiple personality disorder. You see any other 'personalities?'"

"No."

"Keep a good sharp eye out. If there are any, one should surface soon. My understanding is, these things tend to cluster. She under any particular kind of stress lately?"

"Not that I know of."

"Work, maybe?"

I want to say *hell, she loves cutting up people for a living* but I resist that.

"Sam loves puzzles. She sees her work as puzzle-solving. I think she'd want to do it even if they didn't pay her for it."

"Marriage okay?"

I want to say *it was until last night* but I stifle that one too.

"We're fine, Doc. I just don't understand this."

"Well, fact is, me neither," he says. "Not yet, at least. Listen, try this. Try getting her to remember things. Jog her memory. Maybe, if we're lucky, you'll find something to jog her right back again."

I tell him I will, thank him and walk out the door.

Doc's as good as his word. I phone and give them my name at the hospital and a moment later I'm speaking with a receptionist in radiology who gives us an MRI appointment for noon tomorrow.

For lunch she wants peanut butter and jelly.

We've got strawberry and peach preserves. Not jelly but close enough.

I make myself a fried egg sandwich and we eat in front of the TV set. I don't know anything about kid's programming but I figure PBS must have something and they do. It's called CLIFFORD THE BIG RED DOG and it's about…a big red dog. Also a purple poodle named Cleo, a blue hound named Mac and a yellow bulldog named T-Bone.

She giggles occasionally.

There's a commercial for something called DINOSAUR TRAIN which is coming up next. Friendly dinosaurs. Why not? Consider Casper.

But I'm really bone-tired now.

"You be all right out here for a little while? I'm gonna go have a short nap. Or maybe you want a nap too?"

"Nah. I'll stay here, Patrick."

I no sooner hit the bed than I'm asleep.

But I wasn't kidding. It *is* a short nap. Half an hour max.

It's Zoey again. Her toy. That yowl. Rising up from the floor at the foot of the bed.

And Sam's heard it too because here she comes, her brow knit with concern, tucking Teddy under her arm and stooping down to pet her. Zoey flinches slightly, hunkering her shoulders beneath Sam's touch. This is an old cat with arthritic bones. She's stroking too hard.

"Easy," I tell her. "Go softer."

She slows her stroke and lightens her touch. Concentrating. Serious. Much better.

For her reward she gets a purr going.

Against all expectations that short nap's been quite restorative. I feel much better. Maybe I can get a little drawing done.

"How's your TV?"

"Good. Can I watch some more?"

Exactly what I want to hear.

"Sure you can. If you want me I'll be in the study."

"Study?"

"The room with the big table. You know."

"Oh," she says, but it's clear she doesn't, not really It's also clear she doesn't much care. She's into those cartoons.

I get to work.

Samantha, I find, is resisting me today. A cynic might say, well, what do you expect? You've got half of her head blown the hell off. But I've dealt with more difficult problems before. Maybe it's that I've introduced a new character, Doctor Gypsum, a Strangelovian sort of guy in dark glasses and aviator cap whose task at the moment—as it will be in the future—is to put Humpty back together again.

It's weird, though. I have the sense that I'm drawing both characters just fine. He's all angles and she, as usual, is all soft lush contours masking the tensile strength within. But somehow I seem not to be getting the distances right between them on the panels. The balance is off composition-wise. Maybe it's a problem of perspective. They're either too close together—even when he's bending over her apparently dead body he seems too close, almost as though he's inside her in the frame—or they're too far apart. You get the feeling they're so far away he might be shouting.

This isn't like me. I know my shit.

I try it a few different ways and finally I get a page layout I like which seems to accommodate the panels as well as open up or close these distances as the case may be.

Time to go on to the next page.

That one comes easier. I'm into the rhythm of it now.

So into it in fact that when the phone rings it barely registers. Work's like that for me—everything in the real world goes away. I get into this zone where it's just me, line, story and characters. Which is why I need total silence when I work. I need to hear it sing.

But the phone *does* ring and it's only when I hear Lily's voice—not Sam's—politely saying *no, sorry, there's no Sam here, guess you got the wrong number, sorry, that's okay* that I panic, realizing I've momentarily forgotten just exactly who's out there to answer and I race out of the room and into the kitchen just in time to see her cradle the receiver.

"Wrong number," she says.

The phone rings again. She reaches for it but I'm faster.

"Hello?"

"Patrick? Hi."

It's Miriam, Sam's boss. Nice lady.

"I just wanted to check in on Sam," she says. "How's she doing?"

How's she doing? She's fucking *missing* is what I want to say. And thinking that brings me close to tears or hysterical laughter or both, I'm not sure which. I feel like some mad doctor in an old black-and-white horror movie.

She's gone! It's alive!

What I do say is, "just as we thought, it's flu. She's going to have to rest up for a few days, bring down the fever. In fact she's dead asleep now."

"Well, tell her we've got everything covered here. Tell her not to worry. It's been a slow week for axe murders and floaters. Chloe and Bill say hi. You take good care of her, now."

"I will."

"Give her our best."

"I will. 'Bye, Miriam."

I let out a big sigh of relief. We lucked out. She really did figure the first call was a wrong number and not that I'm holding some little girl hostage here out in the boonies.

"Patrick? Whatchu doin' in there anyway? You're quiet."

"Drawing. Want to see?"

Jog the memory.

"Okay."

She follows me into the study. Stands off to one side of the drawing board. But her attention's drawn immediately to the shelves. We keep a lot of books in here, mostly art books and Sam's medical texts. But I've been collecting comic-book and horror action figures for years. I've got Superman, Batman and Robin, Green Hornet, the Mummy, the Wolf Man, Frankenstein, Godzilla, Rodan—there's probably two dozen or more. Hell, I've even got a plastic Jesus.

"You have toys!" she says.

Wide-eyed, like she's never seen them before. So much for memory-jogging in this room.

"Yeah. I guess I do."

"Can I play with them?"

"They're not really for play. More just to look at."

"Oh."

I can tell she's disappointed. Like it or not, right now she's just a kid. And all she's got are some Barbies and Teddy to play with. I point to the drawing board.

"Here, check this out."

I lay out the Samantha pages one by one on the board.

"This is what I do in here."

These are pretty good, I think. Some of the best work I've done. Moody, and with lots of action.

"You do this?"

"Yes. You like it?"

"Yeah. There's no color, though."

"Color comes later."

I keep turning the pages and I can see she's interested.

"It would be better if they moved," she says, "like on TV."

And then she's looking back at the shelves again. Distracted. I'm only halfway through the pages.

I can't help it, I feel a flash of irritation, maybe even anger. And yeah, it's anger, all right. Anger at *Sam. Not at Lily but at Sam.* Sam for doing this. Sam for leaving me. And then anger at myself for feeling that way. It's not her fault.

Is it?

I put the pages down and cover them over.

"Let's go see about dinner. What do you say?"

DINNER IS HOT DOGS AND FRENCH FRIES. HER CHOICE. What did I expect? I zap some beans and saurkraut in the microwave too but she doesn't touch either one, just slathers her dog and fries with ketchup. I've never seen her use ketchup on a hot dog before. Hitherto she's always been a Gulden's mustard girl.

Around a mouthful of fries she says, "it's not fair."

"What's not fair?"

"You've got toys."

"They're not really toys. They're just for show."

She's pouting. "They're toys," she says. "And all I've got is Teddy and some stupid dolls."

"I thought you liked those dolls."

"They're okay, I guess…"

But. I'm not stupid. I get it.

"You want some other stuff, right? Some of the stuff you saw on TV, maybe?"

She brightens right away.

"Yeah!"

"Okay. After we eat we'll go on the net and see what we can find. How's that?"

"The net?"

No memory of the net either. Sam has sites and files saved by the dozens.

"You'll see."

SHE'S FASCINATED BY THE COMPUTER. I REMEMBER reading somewhere that all kids are. At least at first.

We hit the merchandise sites. She's standing behind me pointing out what she likes while I'm punching in the site addresses and clicking on the items. During the next half hour we purchase an Abby Cadabby Bendable Plush Doll, a Once Upon a Monster video game, a knot-a-quilt package, a Teeny Medley bead set, a Stablemate Deluxe Animal Hospital—complete with quarter horse, foal, donkey, goat, resident cat and border collie, operating table and bandage box—and a pair of Curious George pajamas. The pajamas come in kids' and mom's sizes so I've bought the latter. By the time we get to the Easy Bake Oven and Super Pack, she's leaning on my shoulders.

She smells of fresh soap and traces of hot dog.

The Oven and Super Pack alone set me back a hundred dollars but who's counting.

The plush Clifford the Big Red Dog another forty-five. I buy them all and arrange for overnight express delivery.

She yawns. She's having fun of course but for her, maybe, it's getting near bedtime.

She's tired. So she walks around and proceeds to sit on my lap.

"Uh, not a good idea, Lily."

"Why not?" She points at the screen. "I want that," she says.

And I'm not sure I like either of these developments.

What she's pointing to is a Baby Alive Doll. At forty bucks a Baby Alive Doll speaks thirty phrases and comes complete with a dress, a bib, a bowl, a spoon, a bottle, diapers, doll-food products— whatever the hell they might be—and instructions.

I imagine the instructions are useful.

The doll says, "I love you, mommy," and "kiss me, mommy," among other things. Eats, drinks, and wets its diaper.

I'm not sure I like that. I'm also not sure it's wise to have her on my lap. I might have been better off when she distrusted me. Because right now this warm woman's body, my wife's body, is in serious danger of giving me a hard-on.

And this body *thinks* it's about five or six years old.

"You're too heavy," I tell her.

"Am not."

"Are so."

"Am not."

To prove it, I guess, she *wriggles* on me. Bumps gently up and down.

"Off," I tell her. "You want me to buy this or not?"

"Oh, okay." I'm a grouch. A spoil-sport.

She gets up. I buy the fucking doll.

* * *

I'M SITTING IN THE CHAIR IN OUR GUESTROOM watching her sleep. The moon is nearly full and through the window behind me it bathes her face in slants of milky white. The night's unseasonably warm so she's pulled the covers down to just below her waist and I can see her belly between her pajama top and bottom, her navel like a tiny pale button pressing up and down against the mattress cover.

My wife's an outie.

I'm thinking about how we met, eight and half years ago. I'd just landed my first job in the publishing business, as a colorist for Arriveste Ventures—garish, primary-color-only work on their Blazeman line. Nights I was brushing up on my anatomy at the adult ed department at Tulsa Community College and Sam, who already had four years under her belt in the coroner's office, was guest lecturer. Her subject that night, the integumenary system. Skin.

A lot was familiar to me. That skin was the largest organ in the body. That skin was waterproofing, insulation, protection, temperature control, guard against pathogens, all rolled up into one. That skin was the organ of sensation. But there was something she said that I'd never considered before, at least not in the way she put it.

She said that skin *permits* us access to the outside world.

"All the orifices in our bodies," she said, "our eyes, noses, ear canals, mouths, anuses, penises, vaginas, nipples—they're all there and function as they do because skin, by not covering them, allows them free communication with the world which is *not* us. Even our pores exist where they do and where they don't, solely by permission of our skin. Pretty smart stuff, skin is."

That got a laugh. But I thought that this Samantha Martin person was pretty smart stuff too.

And I was already thinking about her own skin.

It had been a year and a half since Linda had e-mailed me from New York saying—apologetically but baldly—that she'd fallen out of love with me. She didn't know why.

Was there another man? No. Something I did or said? No. It just happened. She'd been meaning to tell me for a while now but hadn't gotten up the courage. I was twenty-four years old and we'd been lovers for four of those years. I was still completely crazy over her. Those seven stages of grief they talk about? I went through all seven at once I think, rattling from one to the other like a game of bumper-pool gone berserk. At the end of it, I more or less vowed that love and even sex could wait. Until I was thirty, maybe.

But then here was Sam's skin. The complexion of her face, her bare arms in the sleeveless blouse, her long graceful neck.

It's always been one of her loveliest features. Arguably her best. Winter-pale or summer-tan, it's always seemed to smolder with some warm inner glow, an even interior lighting. There are tiny dances of freckles across her shoulders, hands and forearms. And one beautiful dark mole just to the left of the small of her back.

I didn't get to see the mole that day. But from my desk in the second row of our classroom the rest was pretty clear to me. That she was smart and she was lovely. Neither fact was lost on anybody in the classroom. Especially the guys.

So while I listened carefully to what she had to say about *parting* epidermis, dermis and hypodermis, about scalpels, about where and how to cut in order to get at all that good stuff inside, I was doing some fantasizing too. About what it would be like to touch her.

I hadn't done that in a long time. Touch a woman.

And when her lecture and the Q&A were over I did.

It's always amazed me to hear beautiful women—actresses or models—say that they hardly ever get asked out, that most men are intimidated by them, tongue-tied by their beauty. Me, I just don't get it. That's never been my problem. Maybe it's this artist's eye of mine that just can't help being drawn to beauty, to want to be in its presence as much as humanly possible. Maybe it's because I grew up in a pretty secure family.

Maybe I just don't know any better. Fools do rush in.

But as the class filed out Sam was talking with our teacher, Mrs. Senner. She stood with her back to me, and that gave me all the excuse I needed. I touched her lightly just beneath the shoulder and said *excuse me?* and the smooth warm softness of her skin and firmness within hurtled straight to my brain like a flaming trail of gasoline.

She turned and smiled.

"Sorry to interrupt," I said. "But I've got a couple of questions. Could I maybe buy you two ladies a cup of coffee?"

I was being disingenuous in the extreme. I knew perfectly well that Mrs. Senner always raced home after class to fix supper for her husband, who was just getting off his shift at Tartan Industries. We all did.

She introduced us, said I was one of her better students, and then gracefully declined.

But Sam accepted.

I don't remember much of what we talked about over coffee first and then two glasses of wine each, and the walk back to our respective cars, except that she seemed as interested in the business of making graphic novels as I was in what went on in the autopsy room. More importantly, the current was there. The connection loud and clear.

Later, after our third date and first night in bed, she would tell me that my hand below her shoulder that evening had startled her, gone through her like a shot. She called herself a workaholic and said that after an affair gone south with an older married man it had been a very long time between drinks for her too and that my touch felt to her like a wake-up call from a long dry dreamless sleep.

It was and still is the loveliest thing anyone has ever said to me.

And now I watch her sleep.

I won't cry. Not yet.

I WAKE UP LIKE SOMEBODY'S HIT ME WITH A CATTLE prod.

I wake up horrified.

Zoey's climbed through an open window which should have a screen in it but doesn't and she's out on the ledge of a tenth-floor apartment, looking fascinated by what she sees below and then frightened and finally bewildered and as I'm crossing the room to get to her, carefully, afraid to startle her she tries to turn on the narrow ledge when she should just be backing up the way she came and falls out of sight into space.

I'm instantly awake, stunned, my arms outstretched in front of me, reaching hopelessly for my cat. Inside the dream and right here in my bedroom I've been shouting, both worlds melded into one. Now they break apart. Zoey stares at me from the foot of the bed.

She gets up and meanders over. I scratch her neck and chin and she tilts her head back and closes her eyes, content. When I stop she steps onto my lap and nuzzles my chin. Breakfast time.

"In a minute, baby. Got to piss." I step into my jeans. Tuck in my tee shirt. Habit. It slightly amazes me that I still have habits.

On the way to the bathroom I can hear the TV. Cartoon voices. Lily's already awake.

The guy I see in the mirror disturbs me so I don't dwell on him. I just finish my business and get out of there.

In the living room Lily's kneeling in front of the TV set, watching a commercial for Sid the Science Kid.

She's also naked to the waist.

There's that mole.

She hears me behind her and turns and smiles.

"'Morning, Patrick."

Even after all these years it is wholly impossible not to take in her breasts.

Sam's breasts are small. You can cup one in each hand and not get much overflow. They're quite pale. So pale that in a few places you can see the dim blue traces of vein beneath the flesh, traces of vulnerability I always thought. Her areolae are a very light brown, almost perfectly round and about an inch wide. Her nipples are pink and a quarter-inch long at all times, permanently erect.

And her nipples have a direct phone line to her cunt. I've made her come dozens and dozens of times without ever going below her waist.

If she notices me looking at them she doesn't show it.

"Something wrong?" she says.

"Where's your pajama top, Lily?"

"On the bed. It got hot."

"Why don't you go get it for me, okay?"

"I'm *still* hot!"

"Girls are not supposed to run around with their tops off, Lily."

"Who says?"

"I say. Trust me."

She sighs again. I'm getting used to that sigh. But she gets off her knees and stomps past me toward the bedroom and as she goes by she brushes my bare left arm with her right breast.

I could practically swear she's done this on purpose.

Like she's flouting her body, flirting with me.

But that's impossible. How can she know how this makes me feel? If this were Sam she'd damn well know of course. Sam's very self-aware. But Lily?

The answer is, she can't. She hasn't got a clue. Kneeling there in front of the TV she was the picture of innocence. Brushing against me's just the sullen, pouty thing any kid might do who isn't getting her way.

Forget about it, I tell myself.

Sure.

I'VE SHOWERED AND SHAVED AND DRESSED AND AS I'm cleaning up the dishes she appears in the kitchen doorway.

"What are we doing today, Patrick? Can we go on the 'puter some more?"

"Actually, I need you to get in the shower for me and then get dressed, okay?"

"Ugh! I *hate* the shower!"

No she doesn't.

"Water gets all in my eyes. Can't I do a bath instead?"

It's all the same to me. "Okay. You want to run the water or should I?"

"You do it."

I finish up the dishes and run her a tub, bend over and test the water with my hand.

"Ready," I tell her.

I stand and turn and there she is in front of me, naked, naturally, clueless again, her pajamas in a heap on the floor. *Jesus wept.* I avert my eyes. I pick up her pajamas and get the hell out of there.

Sam is a neat-freak but Lily obviously isn't. Her clothes from the day before lie on the floor of her bedroom where she dropped them in a more-or-less straight line from the door to the bed. Shoes, tee shirt, jeans, panties, socks.

I make her bed and fold her pajamas and put them in a drawer. But for them, the drawer's empty. If this goes on much longer, if Sam's going to be Lily for a while, I should probably move more of her stuff from our room to this one but I'm damned if I'm going to do that right now. We've got this MRI coming up at noon. Nothing changes any more than it has to until I get the results on that.

I pick up her clothes. I lay her jeans out on the bed, the Avia running shoes beneath the bed. The socks and panties go in the laundry basket but that's in the bathroom and I can hear her splashing around in there. I'm not going in. I carry them into our room and select a fresh pair of each, go back to her room and lay them out beside her jeans.

I realize I'm not thinking quite straight. I'm carrying her used socks and panties around instead of just tossing them on my bed until she gets out of there. So that's what I do. Go back to our room and drop them on my unmade bed.

Something catches my eye.

The panties.

Sam says she has little time to shop and she's not like most women anyhow, she doesn't really like shopping. So the panties arrived via UPS from Victoria's Secret along with a half dozen other pairs a few weeks ago. They're ivory. And ivory shows up stains.

There are skid-marks on Sam's panties. Or should I say Lily's.

She hasn't wiped sufficiently.

So now I've got a problem. Do I call her on this or no? If I do it'll likely embarrass her. I don't want to embarrass her. I figure maybe it's a one-shot. I figure I'll spray the damn things with some of our eco-friendly stain remover and leave it at that.

In my red Sierra 4x4 the radio's tuned to our classic rock station—the Band doing THE WEIGHT—and wonder of wonders, Lily's singing along.

"You remember that song?"

"'Course I do."

"You remember any others?"

"I dunno. I guess."

"Which ones?"

"I dunno."

"Name me one."

She shifts uncomfortably in the seat. "Why are we going to the hospital, Patrick?"

"We're going to test something."

"Like in a quiz?"

"Nope. There's a machine that does the testing. All you do is lie down and watch a bunch of pretty lights."

"You too?"

"No, just you this time. I already had my test, a long time ago."

Concussion. I slipped on the ice six or seven years back.

"Did you pass?"

"Yep. And so will you."

I'm trying to sound nonchalant but secretly I'm very worried about how this is all going to go down. For an MRI to work you've got to lie perfectly still— not an easy thing to get a kid to do. The machine is noisy as hell and if you're at all given to claustrophobia this will definitely bring it out in you. An MRI can be a scary creature.

I'm worried about how Lily's going to take it. All sorts of scenarios flit through my head. Lily screaming, crying, banging on the tubing, refusing to lie down, scrambling off the table, hiding. Lily in tantrum.

I know how bad this can get. My first clear childhood memory is of me doing pretty much all of these things when faced with my first hypodermic needle. The doctor was not pleased. I doubt that a radiographer will be either.

Ignorance being bliss though, she doesn't seem at all concerned. She's gazing out the window at the cows and horses out to pasture, the corn stalks, the fields of soy and wheat. We pass a produce store, a used-car lot selling car-ports, the RoundUp Grocery and the River Winds Casino.

Yep, gambling and wheat fields, that's us. There are any number of Indian-owned casinos out here, with names like Buffalo Run and Stables. They're wildly outnumbered by the churches, of course.

But attendance-wise the smart money's always on the Indians.

When we pull in to the parking lot of Baptist Regional Health she's singing along to the Kinks' MISSING PERSONS.

She can remember these songs. But she can't remember me.

WE FIND OUR WAY TO RADIOLOGY AND THE ROOM IS packed. Almost entirely older people. I'm wondering if there's an Early Bird Special on MRIs and CAT-scans these days.

A young woman in Admitting hands me a clipboard and a pen and we find a seat. While I'm filling out the papers Sam's fidgeting, openly staring at all the people around her like she's never seen this kind of crowd before. Fascinated, just short of rude. Across from us a skeletal white-haired woman smiles at her, a little flustered by being stared at you can tell, and Sam smiles back like this woman is her very best friend in the world. The woman hides inside her magazine.

"What's that?"

She's pointing to a guy about my age seated by the wall to our left, wearing overalls and work boots and cradling his right arm up into his chest. Luckily he's talking to the woman beside him—presumably his wife—so he doesn't notice.

"A sling. The man hurt his arm. But it's not nice to point, Lily."

"It's pretty."

She's right. The sling's a deep burgundy, some sort of paisley print.

"You've got one a lot like it. Only yours is blue."

"I have a sling?"

"It's a scarf. You make a sling out of a scarf. Normally you wear it around your neck. Or over your head."

"Can you show me when we get home?"

"Sure."

I finish the paperwork and bring it to the desk. Sam's sort of baby-stepping along behind me. The woman in admitting smiles. "You can go right in," she says.

"Excuse me?"

"They're expecting you. Right through this door."

I knew that Doc had clout but this is amazing.

I open the door for Sam and we're greeted by the radiographer, a short slim guy in hospital scrubs who introduces himself as Curtis. First or last name, I don't know.

"Mr. Burke. Lily. Right this way, please."

Lily?

Samantha was what I wrote on the chart. Talk about greasing the skids. The Doctor has outdone himself this time. He leads us down a corridor and opens a door to our right.

Sam steps inside ahead of me and her eyes go wide.

"It's all white!" she says.

Which it is. The whole room looks like it's made of porcelain. Walls, scanner, scanner bed, chairs, stretcher, linens. Everything except a long wide window directly ahead of us—Curtis' monitoring station.

"Are you wearing any jewelry, Lily?" he asks.

"No."

"What about the ring?"

"Oh, that."

She tugs off her wedding ring and hands it to him.

"Good. Then all you have to do is lie down on your back here and relax."

"She doesn't have to change? No scrubs?"

"Nope. She's good to go as-is."

She hops up on the scanner bed. Curtis plumps her pillow. She lies down.

"It's going to be a little noisy," he says. "Want to listen to some music?"

She nods, smiles. He produces a pair of headphones.

White.

I hear faint muzak coming from them as she puts them on. Sam would have died.

"Would you like to stay, Mr. Burke?"

"I think I'd better, yes."

I'm still apprehensive as to how she's going to take this.

"Then I'll need your watch and your ring. Anything else metal? Any change in your pockets?"

"No."

I hand him the ring and the watch and he turns to Sam again.

"I'm going into that room now, Lily. I'll be able to see you and talk to you and you can talk to me if you need to and I'll hear you—but only if you really, really need to, okay? Otherwise try be real quiet. Like pretend you're sleeping. Try not to move at all, you know? Make believe you're asleep."

She nods again and smiles. This guy is pretty good.

He exits the room. I sit in a chair. A few moments later Sam begins to move. Head first into the belly of the beast.

She's a fucking trooper.

Not a wiggle out of her. A half hour later we're back in the car headed home. And our timing's perfect because as we turn onto the driveway, the long clay road that cuts through our forest, there's a UPS truck just ahead of us.

Or maybe it's not perfect. The driver's going to meet Lily.

Anyway, our toys are here.

The driver's a woman of about forty who I've never seen before, not our usual driver, very pretty even in her baseball cap and oversized drab brown uniform. 'Mornin', she says as she gets out of the truck and we both say 'mornin'. She hauls open the back.

"I've got nine for you today, Mr. Burke, Miz Burke."

"I'm Lily."

"Glad to meet you, Lily."

"What're these?"

"We ordered them, remember? On the computer."

"Toys!" she says.

The driver says nothing but it can't possibly be lost on her that this is not the voice of your normal thirty-something woman. We help her unload. The silence is pretty thick except for Sam, who's humming IT'S NOT EASY BEING GREEN. And I can't help it, I'm embarrassed for her. Or maybe for me, I'm not sure. Either way it sucks.

When we've got them all inside and I've signed for them the driver gives me a smile as she climbs back into the truck but she won't meet my eyes.

"You have a good afternoon," she says.

And I can almost hear her thinking *she's so pretty, too bad she's retarded. And too bad for him too.*

She pulls away. I almost want to throw something. But I don't.

LILY WANTS TO OPEN EVERYTHING RIGHT AWAY BUT it's way past lunchtime so I make us some tuna sandwiches and a pitcher of lemonade and we take them outside to the old stone barbecue and eat at the wooden table there. The sun is glinting on the river. There's the scent of earth and trees and grass growing. It's a relaxing, Saturday-or-Sunday kind of thing to do and Sam and I have done it many times. But Lily just wolfs it down. She really wants at those packages.

"You remember this?" I ask her.

"Remember? 'Member what?"

"This. Doing this. Us being here together."

She shakes her head. "I never did."

* * *

67

It seems to take forever but by the time I've got the animal hospital ready for surgery in the living room, the Easy Bake Oven alive and bake-ready in the kitchen, she's already got the Once Upon A Monster video game running and Teddy and Abby Cadabby are having tea under the watchful eye of her new Baby Alive Doll.

That goddamn doll is spooky.

I figure I've got to log in some drawing time.

I work for maybe an hour, hour and a half but something's wrong again. Now it's Samantha herself who somehow seems to be eluding me on the page. She doesn't look right. I've been drawing this woman for weeks now and know exactly who she is. Hell, I've even put her face and head back together after a shotgun blast.

So what's my problem?

I go back through the first few pages and study her, then flip to today, go to the middle and flip again, back to the first few and flip to yesterday, back and forth until finally I've got it. She's consistent until yesterday, when I had that difficulty with perspective. And today's an extension of what I did yesterday. I'd have seen it then if I hadn't been occupied with composition. It's subtle but it's apparent now.

Sam would have caught it in a minute. I try not to think how much I miss that.

Samantha's gotten slightly slimmer. A little less heft to the breasts, a bit narrower in the hips and thighs. A little more like the real Sam.

More like Lily.

And I'm thinking well, what the hell, fuck it, I can fix that—it's ridiculous and annoying to have to do over the last three pages but it's no big deal and god knows I've been preoccupied with the real Sam so that it's no huge surprise that she'd have crept a bit into my work—I'm thinking this when I hear a crash from the kitchen.

In the kitchen the scene would be funny if it weren't so pathetic. There's Sam at the counter, hands raised in what looks like surrender, her eyes wide and mouth agape like she's just seen a ghost scutter across the floor. Only what's down there is a sodden paper napkin beside some buttery toweling, each of which is soaking up a mixture of what turns out to be flour, baking powder, vanilla, vegetable oil and round red sugar crystals. *Barbie's Pretty Pink Cake.* Which is also all over the tail and haunches of my cat. She's skulking toward the door.

I grab her before she can make her getaway and now it's all over me too for chrissake.

I rush her to the sink.

"Jesus, Sam! What the hell…?"

"My elbow I hit it and it fell and she was there and *I'm not Sam!*"

"Okay you're not Sam goddammit, but gimme a goddamn hand here. Turn on the tap, will you? Warm, please. Not hot."

I can't keep the edge out of my voice and I don't try. What the hell was she thinking, doing this without me being here? My cat hates water unless she's drinking it.

"Here. Hold her here. Around the shoulders."

She does as I say and miraculously Zoey's behaving so I tip a bit of dish detergent into my hands and rub it into a lather, rinse and do it again.

Then I go to work on my cat.

Zoey keeps giving me these disgusted looks until at last I've got her toweled dry and we set her free. Sam hasn't said another word to me through the whole thing.

"Look, I'm sorry I snapped at you," I tell her.

"I'm not Sam. You keep calling me Sam. Why?"

I have no good answer to that. At least none she'd understand.

"You remind me of somebody."

"Who?"

"Somebody I know."

"Is she nice?"

"Yes. Very nice."

This is killing me.

"Let's clean up this mess on the floor, okay?"

"Okay."

At around eight that night I turn the sound off on a show about elephants on NATURE and pull out the photo album. We stopped taking photos a few years back for some reason, but there we are in the old days just after we met, Sam thirty and me twenty-eight in front of the Science Museum, taking in the fireworks at Carousel Park, down by the Falls, Sam on a bench in City Park, waving at me.

"She does look a lot like me," she says.

I say nothing.

There are three pages of photos I took at the St. Augustine Alligator Farm back in our 2008 vacation and these seem to fascinate her. The crocks and turtles, the albino alligators, the wild bird rookery, the Komodo Dragon. She's forgotten Sam entirely.

I turn to some of the older family photos. My mother and father, my brother Dan, her parents on her father's birthday. She doesn't seem interested in these at all.

"They're nice," she says. "Can we watch the elephants?"

I'm awakened by Lily's voice.

"Patrick? I'm scared."

She's turned on the light in the hall behind her and she's standing in the doorway in her Curious George pajamas, hands and cheek pressed to the doorjamb like she's hugging it. I'm still woozy from sleep but through the open window I can hear what's bothering her.

Above the chirping of crickets, the wind's whipping the howling and yipping of a pack of coyotes across the river. They'll try to take cows down now and then over there and they tend to like to celebrate when they do. There seem to be a lot of them tonight, and the mix is eerie, from the long sonorous wolf-like wail of the adults to the staccato *yip yip yip* of the young. Which sounds for all the world like demented evil laughter.

Even the crickets sawing away in the darkness sound vaguely sinister tonight.

No wonder she's scared. Even to my ears it's spooky.

She looks so vulnerable standing there. Shoulders hunched, legs pulled tight together, her thumbnail pressed against her upper front teeth. More like a kid in some ways than I've yet seen her. So much less of Sam, so much more of Lily.

Almost like the daughter we'll never have.

"It's okay. It's just a bunch of coyotes. They can't hurt you. They're way out there over across the river."

"Patrick?"

"Yeah?"

"I'm scared."

"I know you're scared but you don't have to be. To them it's a kind of music, like singing, only because we're not them, it sounds weird, a little scary. That's all."

"Singing?"

"Uh-huh."

"I don't like it."

"Try to go back to sleep, Lily. They really can't hurt you. Honest."

"Can I...could I stay with you, Patrick?"

I want her to. I don't want her to.

Contradictions slam together.

"You'll be fine over there, Lily."

"No I won't."

"Sure you will."

"No I won't. I'll be good, I promise. I won't wriggle around or anything. I promise."

I can hear the tremble in her voice. Almost like a desperation there. She really is scared.

"Okay," I tell her. I scoot over to the far side of the bed by the window. She scampers to the bed as though the floor's on fire and hops in. Throws the light summer bedcovers over her shoulders and snuggles up next to me. She's shaking.

It's automatic. I put my arm around her and then her head is resting on my shoulder.

I haven't done anything like this for days.

It makes me almost light-headed.

It's as though this is Sam again, as always. As though nothing's changed. But one thing reminds me that everything's changed.

Her hair.

When Sam comes to bed and we hold one another close like this I'm always aware of the faint traces of shampoo in her hair, Herbal Essence or Aussie Mega. It's a clean smell, as familiar to me as the scent of her breath or the feel of her skin beneath my hand.

Lily hasn't shampooed today.

It's not a bad smell, just flat and slightly musky. But it's not Sam's smell, not at all.

I'll have to remind her in the morning. Shampoo your hair.

Meantime, if I close my eyes, the rest of her is Sam. My hand on her arm, her cheek on my shoulder, her leg against mine.

Lily keeps her promise. She doesn't wriggle.

But it's a long time before I'm able to sleep. And it isn't the coyotes.

* * *

IN MY DREAM I'M TELLING SOMEBODY OR OTHER AT somebody's dinner table how extraordinary I think it is that I'll die someday, just disappear tonight or tomorrow or whenever, and I'm wondering out loud just what will disappear along with me when I do. I awake with a raging hard-on tenting up the covers and a sense of puzzlement that one should somehow coincide with the other.

Mercifully Lily's already up.

It makes no real sense and actually the thought's briefly annoying but I'd rather she not see this. So I peer out into the hallway to make sure the coast is clear before I head for the bathroom. Then standing there peeing I wonder if she's *already* seen it. It's possible.

The call from Doc Richardson comes at nine-thirty.

"She tested out just fine, Patrick. Is she still…?"

"Yeah. She's still Lily."

I don't know whether to be relieved or not. If it were a brain-thing it might be treatable. But then again…

He sighs. "Well, there's nothing physically wrong with her. Everything looks perfectly normal. Have any other personalities appeared?"

"No."

"And no sign of Sam at all, I assume."

"None."

"Then I think you need to have her see a therapist. I'm out of my league here. But I know a good one. Have you got a pen?"

I write down the woman's name, address and phone number. I do it mostly for the doc's sake. I'm pretty sure I'm not going to use the information. Call it pride or stubbornness—I want to see this through on my own if I can. I'll keep it by the phone as a last resort.

"Thanks for what you did at the hospital, Doc."

"My pleasure. Hey, they owe me. Good luck with the therapist. And keep me posted, all right? You know I'm very fond of Sam."

"I know. I will." I thank him and hang up.

I'm thinking that with or without a therapist, this could take a while.

Lily's on the couch, nibbling from a box of raisin bran. Her left arm's poking out of a paisley scarf. Her sling. Herman the Human Cannonball is about to be launched by the gang over at Sesame Street.

"Lily, as soon as the show is over I want you to run a tub for your bath, okay? And be sure to wash your hair. You forgot yesterday."

"Okay."

She doesn't seem the least distressed so I'm guessing she missed the woody.

I go back to the phone and speed-dial the coroner's office.

"Miriam, hi. It's Patrick Burke. Listen, I wasn't being completely truthful when we spoke. In fact I wasn't telling you the truth at all—I don't know why. There's no flu. Never was. Physically, Sam's fine. This is…something else…"

"You mean like a breakdown?"

"I guess that's what you'd call it, yes."

"God, I'm so sorry, Patrick. Are you all right? I mean…"

"The two of us are fine, Miriam. Well, we'll *be* fine once she gets through all this. But I'm afraid I'm going to have to ask you to give her a leave of absence for a while."

"Absolutely. You take all the time you need. Your wife works like a soldier. She deserves it. Can I speak with her? Would that be okay, do you think?"

"I don't think so. She's pretty fragile at the moment. Maybe in a week or so."

"Is she seeing somebody, getting therapy?"

"Yes."

Two lies inside of twenty minutes. Not bad, Patrick. I give her the therapist's name just to seal the deal.

"Good. Well, give Sam my best, will you? From all of us. And if there's anything I can do…"

"I will."

And that lie makes three.

I'M AT THE DRAFTING TABLE WORKING ON SAMANTHA duking it out with The Torque, trying to keep her from going all svelte on me again, when I'm aware that the television's gone off and there's water running in the tub. A little while after that I can hear her splashing around in there. She's left the door open.

"Lily?"

"Yeah."

"Close the door. And don't forget to wash your hair!"

"You do it."

"What?"

"You do it. I get soap in my eyes."

"No you don't."

"I do too. You do it, Patrick."

She'll be naked in there.

I tell myself that I'm being silly. That's my wife in there and I've seen her naked thousands of times. *Get a grip, Patrick.*

"All right. I'm coming."

I finish crosshatching Torque's ugly mug, get up and walk to the bathroom.

She's sitting in soapy water up to her breasts, small peaked islands in the waves. Beneath the water I can see her pubic hair. She hasn't depilated in a while so it drifts like tiny dark strands of seaweed. Her left thigh is under water but her right leg's bent so she can get at the toes, which she's soaping vigorously. It tickles. She giggles. Her thigh gleams.

There's a small line of soap like soul patch on her chin so I wipe it off with my finger.

"You ready?"

"Uh-huh."

"Duck under."

She tilts her head back into the water and comes up sputtering, wiping her eyes. Meanwhile I've got the shampoo off the shelf. I pour some into the palm of my hand and smooth it into both hands, kneel beside the tub and work it into her smooth fine hair. She smiles at me.

"Don't get it in my eyes, Patrick."

"I won't."

And I'm careful not to. But I can't help thinking of our last real night together, starting with our shower, starting with me shampooing her hair just as I'm doing now.

Then telling her *turn around, I'll do your back.*

She does. I wash her back, her ass, her breasts, her stomach. She raises her arms and I wash her armpits, her arms, then her back and ass again, into the crack of her ass, into her cunt. She soaps her own hand and reaches down to me.

This is not a good place to go.

She's looking up at me with those very innocent eyes.

I turn on the water behind her. Fiddle with the hot and cold until it's luke.

"Okay, rinse. Close your eyes." I'm trying to keep the thickness out of my voice.

I cup my hands, collect the fresh tap water and pour. Collect and pour. Over and over again until her hair is clean and shiny. She stands up, raises her arms and smoothes her hair back off her forehead. The gesture is so *Sam* it floors me for a moment but only for a moment because with her arms raised I can see the dark stubble in her armpits. Three days growth now. Sam shaves every day.

I wonder if Lily's noticed.

WHILE SHE'S TOWELING OFF I GO INTO HER ROOM and retrieve yesterday's tee shirt, socks and panties.

The panties are stained again, worse than before. I'll have to talk to her.

"DAD?"

"Pat? Hey, how are you?

My father is Daniel Patrick Burke and he and my mother are the only people in the world allowed to call me Pat.

I don't phone him nearly enough. But he's good about it. I think he understands.

"I'm okay. How about you?"

"Not bad. Got a little golf in this morning. I'll never be any good at the damn game but it gets me off my butt now and then. My partner was Bill Crosby. He asked about you, sends his best."

Bill always does. Like my father he's a retired schoolteacher. Only my father taught math in Tulsa while Bill taught history in the Bronx. Bill's a little rougher around the edges.

"Tell him I said hi."

"I will."

There's a pause on the other end and I hear the flick of a lighter. My father's Zippo. My dad's got emphysema. He shouldn't be smoking at all but he figures half a pack a day will buy him a little more time than two packs would. He's content to leave it at that for now.

"How's the weather been?"

"You know, sunny Sarasota. Weather's fine. I just wish the snowbirds would hurry up and go home. You can't get a parking space anywhere in this damn town. I went to visit your mother yesterday and then decided to grab a bite to eat. I had to walk five blocks to the Bonefish Grille and then waited half an hour for a table. Sometimes I think everybody down here's from Minnesota."

So here comes the inevitable. The dreaded question. The reason I don't call too often. But I have to ask.

"How's mom?"

I hear him pull hard on his Winston.

"She asked me who I was, Pat."

He lets it lie there a moment. On this end, I'm frozen.

"Sometimes she knows me and sometimes she doesn't. I wanted to take her out for some ice cream. You know she loves ice cream. They tell me that's typical. That with Alzheimer's the sweet tooth goes last. But she gets so confused, you know? She wanted to get a sweater even though I told her she didn't need one. She couldn't find her own clothes closet. She went looking in the bathroom."

My father knew he needed to put his wife of forty-two years in a managed care facility when she decided to make a frozen pizza for a snack one night and put the pizza in the oven, box and all.

"Anyhow I got her out of there and we went for a drive and I got her her chocolate sundae. She seemed to enjoy herself, to have a good time. She even reached over and smiled and had some of my banana split, just like a little kid. She was sweet. But, you know, she never once asked about you or your brother. And I'm not sure she knew who I was, even when I kissed her goodbye. Even then she looked puzzled."

He sighs, coughs. After two years this is still always rough for him. He changes the subject.

"You hear anything from your brother?"

"No."

And now the pause is on my end. My brother Ed is two years older than me—he became a D.C. cop after the Marine Corps. He thinks what I do for a living is ridiculous. I think what he does is probably just short of criminal.

Besides, I'm thinking about Sam.

"Something wrong, son?"

"No, dad. Everything's fine. I'm just a bit tired, that's all."

"How's Sam?"

"Sam's fine. She's glued to the television."

Which is true. I just don't tell him what show it is.

"Give her my love, will you."

"Sure, dad. Of course I will."

Another pause from me. I'm picturing my mother and her chocolate sundae, her reaching across the table.

"You sure you're okay, Pat?

And I almost tell him then. I almost blurt out the entire thing, because I love my father and maybe he can comfort me, maybe he can tell me it's going to be all right and make me believe him the way I always believed him when I was young and he was the dad, the schoolteacher you could always go to, who always knew that you treated kids the same as you treated adults, with respect and an open heart.

I want to tell him that I miss her—that I miss *us*. Because we've always been one hellova pair, Sam and I, not just lovers but the best friends either of us has ever had, who tell one another when we're hurting or need help and love to crack one another up with some silly goddamn joke. We love the same cat. Respect the same books. Smile to the same Tom Waits CDs in the car. Share a grave distrust of politics, lawyers and Wall Street.

I want to tell him that I feel abandoned. Like part of me's living alone.

But my mother's burden enough for him.

"I'm fine, dad. Honest."

I can't tell if he buys that or not. Finally he breaks another silence.

"Okay. The two of you come visit your old dad one day soon, all right? It's been too long."

"Sure, dad. We will. I promise. Love you."

"Love you too, son. Love to Sam. 'Bye."

OVER THE NEXT TWO WEEKS I SLASH AWAY AT Samantha. I'll tame that lovely bitch, keep her juicy ass big if it takes everything I've got. My deadline's not until the end of next month but when I'm not with Lily I'm obsessive about this. The pages don't exactly fly—I keep having to correct them—but I'll have it done way before then.

We've fallen into a kind of pattern, Lily and I. She fixes her own cereal in the morning and I make lunch and dinner. I work while she plays. I make sure she has a bath every day and—over her protests, at first—that she washes her own damn hair. Once was quite enough for me. I order out for groceries. I do the laundry, skid marks and all. Can't seem to bring myself to talk to her about that.

But Lily's meanwhile become more demanding. Can't blame her. She's bored. Television and beads can only go so far. Same for Barbie's two-story Glam Vacation House, Glam Convertible and Glam Pool and Slide. For a few days she's into her Easy Bake Oven. She masters Barbie's Pretty Pink Cake and goes on to Snow Mounds, Raisin Chocolate Chip Cookies, S'Mores, and Easy Bake Brownies.

All a bit sweet for me. But I pretend to like them fine.

Her Baby Alive Doll likewise exerts its pull. Temporarily. She feeds it, bottles it, listens to its inane prattle and changes its diapers. Teddy seems to be acting as surrogate daddy for a while but I sense his ultimate discouragement. Baby Alive is so screamingly *dull*.

The weather's been fine. She wants to go outside, meet other kids. She wants to go out and play.

But other kids are out of the question.

When she asks me why, I tell her that you have to go to school to meet other kids and she's not going to school right now. Which puzzles her. But for a while at least she lets it lie.

Zoey wants to go outside too from time to time I think. Always has. I'll see her gazing out the window, chattering at the birds, or else she'll be peering around my legs at the door. But there are critters out there who'd be all too happy to tear her limb from limb.

There are critters of the two-legged variety who'd do the same for Sam.

Re-tard.

There's an old rusty swing set and slide left here by the previous owner over by the side of the house. We never use it. But now I set it in order for her. I sand down the rust on the slide, steps, chains and wooden seats and test the chains. I oil the hangers. I have to solder one of the hangers and two links on the chains but other than that it's in remarkably good shape.

I buff the slide with SOS pads, hose it down to a shine and test it out myself. I land hard on my ass, which makes Lily laugh. *I'll have to get some sand.* She lands gracefully of course on both feet and giggling, on a run.

Never mind the sand.

She's happy to be out. Happy with the swing set in particular. Some days she wants me to push her so I do and it's a curious feeling. It's like I'm playing two roles here at the same time, parent or playmate to the kid who shouts *higher, higher*—but then in our quieter moments it's almost romantic, like we're a new pair of lovers again, doing the kinds of silly kid-things that lovers do.

I think of Sam and me at the amusement park in Kansas City years ago, before we were married, the way she kissed me from a bobbing horse when I managed to grab that brass ring.

* * *

THEN THERE'S THE RIVER.

She wants to know if it's okay to go swim in the river.

There are water moccasins and snapping turtles in there. Snappers are shy usually but water moccasins can be aggressive as hell. They'll swim right at you. Sam knows enough to look out for them but would Lily? Lily would not. I figure I can be her eyes, though. She wants to swim. It's hot. We've got a dock. Might as well use it.

I still haven't gotten around to transferring Sam's clothes to Lily's room so I go into her drawer and pick out Sam's favorite two-piece. Cobalt blue. When last seen wearing it she was making guys stumble into their wives at the bar at the Pelican Grove Palms.

While she's putting it on in her bedroom I pack a cooler with a couple of cold Pepsis for her and three Coronas for me and slap together two bologna and cheese sandwiches. I'm not sure I'm all that hungry but I can always feed the crappie with mine when she's finished swimming.

"Patrick?"

I'm wrapping sandwiches. "Uh-huh?"

"Could you do this?"

She's standing with her back to me. She's got her sandals and bottoms on but the halter's hanging loose from her shoulders.

There's that mole again.

Did I mention that her back comes complete with the Dimples of Venus? Two deep indents on either side of her backbone down low at her hips. I snap together her halter.

"There. You ready? Got the towels?"

"Yup."

We make a stop at the tool shed. Against the possibility of water moccasins I select a rake with steel tines. You never know.

She's all nervous excited energy. Practically jumping up and down. She runs ahead of me out to the dock and before I've even gotten there she's cannonballed into the silty water. She surfaces smiling and wipes her face and sputters.

"How's the water?"

"It's *freezing!*" Maybe it is, but not enough to stop her.

The water on the river moves with a slow steady current here but she swims easily back to the dock, turns and swims out a bit further and then back again and holds onto the dock kicking her feet behind her and I realize that it's Sam's crawl I've been watching. She remembers perfectly how to swim.

I almost say something but I don't. Every time I've spoken Sam's name the reaction hasn't been good.

So I shut up and watch my wife swim.

WE DO THIS NEARLY EVERY DAY WHEN THE weather's good. I'm not about to let her swim in a storm. I have to explain to her about lightning. I don't go in myself, I just sit on the dock with my rake and my cooler and watch her and watch for snakes. I was raised around chlorine swimming pools, and natural water—lakes, rivers, oceans—just don't seem right to me.

I do like to fish, though. And crappie are great eating.

I dig out the fishing rods and the tackle box. Besides crappie, my favorite, you can pull bass and perch from the river. Catfish, of course, if you're bottom fishing. And gar, which look like fucking prehistoric monsters and are vicious on the line. Their bodies are heavily armored and their jaws are filled with long sharp teeth. You catch a gar, you don't touch the damn thing, you cut away the hook, leave it to him as a souvenir. I've seen gar with three or four of them hanging from their jaws like some kind of Goth mouth-jewelry.

You can use practically anything as bait—chicken liver, frozen shad, dough balls—but I prefer nightcrawlers myself. There's a ravine about a half mile from the house and at night after a heavy rain there are hundreds of pale fat bodies wriggling through the grass trying to keep from drowning. All you need is a flashlight and a jar with a perforated lid and some dirt inside and you'll have your bait in no time.

So that's what we do.

Sam never liked this part. I mostly did it alone. But Lily's delighted at discovering this strange living world writhing under our flashlights at her feet. Even more so at finding some of them stuck together. I'm not going to try to explain to her about hermaphroditism.

She has no problem at all picking one up, examining up-close and then dropping in the jar.

The problem comes the following day when we start to fish.

She *hates* worming the hook. Won't have any part of it. Hates to watch me doing it too.

She's feeling the worm's pain.

I always wondered exactly how much pain is really involved in this. It's not as though a worm has much in the way of a nervous system. But it's important to push the hook through the flesh of the worm several times so it doesn't slip off in the water. Usually three will do. But after the first invasion of that flesh the writhing can get pretty intense. As though the worm were angry, indignant at this unwarranted piercing. You can look at the worm and imagine you're seeing torture up close and personal.

Lily really can't stand to watch. So our fishing expedition is a short one. We go home with a perch and two crappies.

I guess that'll do.

WHEN DOC CALLS I'M UNPREPARED FOR IT.

It's past 10:00 a.m. I've just gotten up. I've slept late again. I'm on my first cup of coffee. Yesterday was our grocery delivery and some of the Frosted Flakes Lily requested are scattered across the kitchen table. Bowl's in the sink, though, so I suppose that's something.

"I just spoke with Trish Cacek," he says.

Doctor Cacek. The shrink.

"She says you haven't brought her in."

"No. I haven't."

"Why's that?"

"I want to wait and see, Doc. See if she comes back on her own."

"I'd advise against that, Patrick. She needs to be in therapy. You seeing *any* improvement at all?"

"Sometimes a look, a gesture. She was yelling in her sleep a few nights ago and I could swear the voice was Sam's. But you know, we don't sleep in the same room anymore, in our room, and by the time I got there she was asleep again."

He sighs. "Take her to Dr. Cacek, Patrick. You can't do this alone. You're too close to it. How are *you* holding up, anyway?"

"I'm fine."

I'm staring at the Frosted Flakes.

"I'm really just fine. We're doing stuff together. Things we used to do. We watched SLEEPLESS IN SEATTLE night before last. One of her favorite movies."

"And?"

"Well, she paid attention. Smiled at the end."

"I'll say this once again. You're too close to this. It's not good for either of you. Get her into therapy."

"I'll think about it, Doc. Honestly I will. I want to try, though, just a little while longer. Thanks for calling. Appreciate it."

We hang up. I wipe down the table. Sit and drink my coffee.

I'm unprepared for the second call too. It's not a half hour later. I'm just finishing up the dishes.

"Hello?"

"Hi, Patrick."

"Oh. Hi, Miriam."

"How are you? How's she doing?"

"Better. A little better, maybe."

"Good. That's great. Can I say hi? Just a quick hello? And I promise not to talk shop."

"I don't think so, Miriam."

For a moment I'm tempted to put Lily on the line. Miriam's a good lady but she's being nosy. I can hear it in her voice. Two minutes with Lily would give her plenty to talk about down at the office.

And now Zoey's standing in the kitchen doorway, yowling, her toy—her little stuffed tuxedo-cat—sprawled at her feet. Thought I'd hid the damn thing.

"Good god, what's that?"

"Our cat, Zoey. She does this sometimes."

"Sounds like somebody's murdering her. So, can I talk to Sam?"

Insistent. Zoey's insistent too.

"Not a good time, Miriam."

"Will you have her call me, then? We're concerned about her."

"I know. Wait. What do you mean?"

"We're…concerned. That's all."

"I'm taking care of her, Miriam. I'm not holding her prisoner or anything."

"I didn't mean…of course you're not. Just…have her call me when she's up to it, okay?"

"Yes. Fine. I will. 'Bye."

I reach down and grab up the toy. Zoey gives one last long yowl as it disappears behind my back and into the pocket of my jeans.

I don't know whether it's Miriam's call or Doc's call or Zoey's whining or all three of them together but right now I'm boiling.

I take a few deep breaths and sit back down at the kitchen table. Zoey ambles over.

It's not her. It's never her. I stroke her fur.

I just touch her.

LILY'S OUTSIDE PLAYING WITH HER BARBIES IN THE sandbox I built for her, pretending it's a beach and the girls are out sunbathing drinking pina coladas or whatever Barbies drink these days while I'm at the drafting table trying to figure out what the hell is wrong here. *Everything* looks wrong to me now, not just Samantha's look and Doctor Gypsum's and the various loathsome members of the Abominations' League but perspective again, the framing of the panels strikes me as flat, dull, something I could have done better twenty years ago. I'm well into the third act and it's just not working for me.

I keep thinking of that conversation with Miriam. *I'm not holding her prisoner or anything.* Where the fuck did that come from? Why did I have to say that?

Screw this. This isn't going anywhere.

I lean out the window.

"Hey Lily! Want to go for a swim?"

She looks up, seems unsure at first. Maybe I was a little loud there.

"Okay, Patrick."

"Suit up."

Skippy peanut butter and Smucker's Concord Grape this time. I've got them wrapped and packed away in the cooler along with the beer and Pepsi but still no Lily.

She's not in her room. She's not in the bathroom. I peer into mine. Found her.

"What's up, Lily?"

She's been in the bedroom drawers. Sam's drawers. She holds an orange and yellow two-piece out to me.

"Could I wear this one instead of the blue?"

"Whatever one you want."

"This one's pretty."

"Well. You should wear it, then."

She opens the closet door. Sam's closet. Fingers a strapless blue and white silk dress. Sam bought it in New York City.

"All this stuff," she says. "It's really, really pretty. Do you think I could play dress-up later, maybe?"

There's a buzzing in my head. A disconnect. I think she says something else to me. I'm not sure.

"What?"

"Later maybe, Patrick? After the swim?"

"I...I guess so. Yeah, if you want. All right. Go put on your suit."

She hurries out of the room and I'm left standing there looking at Sam's clothes hanging neatly in the closet and disheveled where Lily's been pawing through the open drawers.

I'll straighten them out. Only not just now.

* * *

I'M HALFWAY THROUGH MY FIRST BEER WHEN I SEE the snake.

The beer hits the deck and I'm up on my feet with the rake in my hands and it's coming toward her, its body a black undulating streak in the water behind a raised head as it rises over a drifting branch and she doesn't see it, doesn't even know it's there and I'm yelling *Sam! Lily! Get out of the water! Get out of the water NOW!* and she hears the panic in my voice and looks confused but starts swimming anyway, Sam's powerful stroke, yet the damn thing's gaining on her, no more than ten feet away.

Faster, Lily! I yell and bless her she really pours it on so that she hits the side of the dock and starts to hoist herself up just as it raises its fucking head to strike but I lash it with the steel tines of the rake. It writhes furiously in the roiling water and tries to bite, the snow-white mouth hitting the wooden handle just above the tines and Lily's out of the water now watching wide-eyed as I flip the rake around and bring it down again and again on its back, on its goddamn head until at last the snake's had enough and turns and glides away.

I drop the rake as though it's poisonous.

I'm shaking so hard it's hard to stand so I don't even try. I drop down beside her on the dock, our feet dangling over the muddy water. Lily pulls hers in as though that thing still might be out there somewhere.

The look on her face is pure shock. She reaches out for me and I reach out for her and then I'm hugging her wet body tight to mine and we're both of us trembling in a sudden cold wind of our own devise.

"Anything I want?"

"Uh-huh."

It's about two hours later and Lily's at the bedroom closet. Seems she's forgotten all about the snake. I sure haven't.

Sam's got a half dozen conservative suits for work front and center in the closet but she pushes those aside to get at the more interesting stuff in back.

She turns to the drawers and opens and closes them one at a time, inspecting them.

"You go 'way now," she says. "I'll come when I'm ready."

I grab a beer from the fridge and plant myself on the couch in front of the TV and watch a rerun of BONES and I think how Sam used to enjoy that show, even though it was utter hokum—the day a medical examiner partnered up with a detective in the field was the day Wall Street worried about ethics.

But that was part of the fun. That and snappy dialogue and the charisma and chemistry of the two leads. I think about us early on, Sam and I, when we first started dating . How people used to say that when we walked in, we lit up the room.

My understanding is that mismatched clothing is all the rage with the kids these days but when she comes out grinning with a flourish and a *ta-da!* I can't help it, I have to laugh. She's got on woolen knee-socks, one green with yellow polka dots, one blue and red with alternating wide stripes. She's teetering on a pair of black brushed leather three-inch heels. The dress is shiny red satin, sleeveless, with a scoop neck, cut to just above the knee. Ralph Lauren. I was with her in Tulsa when she bought it.

She's wearing Sam's three-strand, nickel and black agate necklace, her turquoise necklace, her red coral necklace and her fossil bead necklace, a brown and yellow camouflage-pattern silk scarf, and a pair of long white gloves with pretty much every ring in Sam's drawer slipped over them. And to top it all off, Sam's wide-brimmed floppy straw sunhat.

"Well?" she says.

"You look…stunning," I manage.

"You like it? You like my shoes? You like my dress? You like my hat?"

"I like all of it."

And I do. Just not necessarily all at the same time.

She turns around and back again a couple of times just like they do on the TV fashion shows I guess. A kind of awkward pirouette.

"Wait! I'm gonna do it again."

She half-rushes, half-staggers back to our bedroom.

I think about her put-together, about what she's selected. At first it makes me smile and then I realize something. Together they're all wrong. Together they're the Clash of the Titans.

But each piece individually is one of Sam's favorites. Every one.

I picture her standing with the bedroom door closed gazing into the full-length mirror on the door, choosing her selections. I asked her once, a week or more ago, what she sees when she looks into a mirror. Wondering, did she see a little girl? *"Me, silly,"* she said and shrugged and wouldn't say anything further.

But what's she seeing now? Bits of Sam? Bits of Sam's history, her likes and dislikes, her memory?

It gives me an idea. I go hunting around in our collection of DVDs until I find it. A couple of years ago we converted a box full of VCR tapes, early home movies, to DVD. Since the photo album was such a flop I'd never bothered to play them for her. But what if it were all a matter of timing? What if she simply wasn't ready then? What if she is now?

It's exciting. Definitely worth a shot.

I key up the DVD player and wait.

WHEN SHE COMES OUT I'M FLOORED AGAIN. BUT this time I'm not laughing.

Her wedding dress. It was in a box on the top shelf in the closet.

She's standing in front of me in her wedding dress.

All the jewelry's gone except our wedding ring which she's been wearing all the time throughout all of this and seems to think nothing of, like it's part of her. But she's looking strangely shy. As though the dress has power, as though the dress has tamed her somehow.

It's floor-length, lace, with delicate spaghetti straps and a modest train. It's supposed to hug her body from breasts to hips but it doesn't quite do that because Lily's not managed the buttons up top. She's holding the veil out to me.

"What's this for, Patrick?" she says.

It's a moment before I can speak. I go to her and take the veil.

"It goes in your hair. Like this."

I arrange the comb in her hair and spread the veil down first over her face which makes her smile and wrinkle her nose and then back over her back and shoulders. I step away.

"You look…beautiful."

"I do?" She's delighted.

"Yes, you do. And you don't know that, do you."

"Know what?"

"That you're beautiful."

"You think?"

"I think."

She looks at me. Her expression serious all of a sudden.

Then, "you're silly, Patrick," she says, and turns to head back to the bedroom.

"Wait. Come here. Sit down a minute. I want to show you something."

I pick up the remote to turn on the DVD player while she sits down next to Zoey curled up on the couch. The dress slides up a bit. I see that she's barefoot.

Zoey seems to regard her lap and the dress as a possible nesting place but apparently decides she's comfortable where she is.

"You need anything? A Pepsi or anything?"

"Nope."

"I'm gonna go grab a beer. Wait right here, okay?"

"Okay."

I do and she does.

I've orchestrated our home videos with old rock and country songs and the occasional show tune. I know exactly where I want to go with this because there she is beside me on the couch, sitting there *in her goddamn wedding dress* so I fast-forward through our first trip to the Big Apple with Gene Kelly and Frank Sinatra and Jules Munshin squeaking their way through *New York New York it's a wonderful town* and there's the Empire State Building and the Chrysler Building and Sam eating a huge pastrami sandwich at the Carnegie Deli and gazing out over the city from the second of the doomed Twin Towers and then we hit the fireworks here in Tulsa, our first fourth of July together, and she says *wait, stop.*

I hit play. Fireworks bore me to tears now though not as much back then. But Lily's interested. The music is the Beatles' FOR THE BENEFIT OF MR. KITE which is something, at least. Still, I want to get on with it. I let her watch for a while and then fast-forward again. And there we are at Yellowstone, "where hell bubbles up," and Tom Petty's singing SAVING GRACE sounding like Alvin's Chipmunks while we're viewing gysers and waterfalls, pools of emerald water and turquoise water, incredible sunsets—and from a distance, a herd of grazing bison. There's Sam in her cutoffs in the foreground, smiling and pointing out at them.

Next we're in Kansas City at Worlds of Fun Amusement Park. There she is opposite me on the Ferris Wheel, on her bobbing yellow horse on that merry-go-round where I snagged the ring, screaming bloody murder on the roller coaster and *wait wait wait go back!* Lily says so I rewind to the roller coaster again, my aim with the video camera jiggly as hell, Willie Nelson doing ON THE ROAD AGAIN while Sam screams silent screams and Lily giggles beside me.

The giggling unnerves me. I want her to wake up, snap out of it. That's what this is for. Instead she's giggling.

The bumper cars are next. *Ooooo* she says, and claps her hands, fascinated, so I know there's no point in fast-forwarding. She'll only want to go back again.

She's pulled the veil down over her face and she's chewing on it absent-mindedly.

On the screen Sam's getting battered from all sides. She's getting creamed. I remember this. Sam was talking to another woman, a parent, about something or other while we were standing in line waiting to ride. There were a bunch of kids behind me, maybe ten of them, all ages, and I turned and got their attention, waving my arms and then pointing to Sam and mouthing *get her!* which made them laugh.

And which they did.

When the segment's over Sam and I are at Broken Bow Lake and it's beautiful and Sam's in her cobalt blue two-piece but I want to get through this so I fast-forward through Roy Orbison's BLUE BAYOU and finally we're there.

At the wedding.

And I'm wondering, does this have a chance in hell of beating out the bumper cars?

But it's uncanny, it's as though I knew back then when I was putting this video thing together that this was going to be important someday. Because I've emphasized it. I've left it utterly, completely silent. No scoring. Just us.

It's a professional behind the camera so the shots are tight, focused, not jittery like my own. So there we are on this nice sunny July day in front of St. John's Episcopal, my own limo pulling up first and me getting out in my tux with my best man McPheeters, both of us grinning, the three Johnny Walkers doing their work on us, and even my brother is smiling for a change, saying something that my groomsmen Joe Manotta and Harry Grazier seem to find actually funny.

It cuts to my mom and Sam's mom being seated by the ushers and I look to her for some sign of recognition but there isn't any, none at all. Next thing I'm standing at the altar with McPheeters watching my brother, Joe and Harry escort Miriam and Sam's two pretty college roommates down the aisle, trailed by our cute little flower girl—I forget her name—very serious about the business of tossing her rose petals *just so.*

Then the moment I'm waiting for. Sam, arriving in front of the church and stepping out of her limo and then beaming on her father's arm, *in the dress,* moving slowly down the aisle.

It's hard to look away but I do. I need to watch Lily.

And I'm rewarded.

She leans forward, intent. She's hardly blinking. She lifts the veil.

I remember this part from the tape. The photographer actually irritated her father slightly by focusing almost entirely on his daughter's face. Almost nothing of him or the priest or the actual ceremony. Even I got short shrift. But I never could blame the guy. It was no wonder he was captivated. Sam was standing bathed that day in a single streak of gentle flame-red light, glowing through a stained-glass window.

This is what Lily's seeing.

I glance at the screen. I know what's next. The ring. The kiss.

I don't watch the kiss but Lily does. She looks puzzled. Her eyes go to me and then back to the screen and her lips seem almost to be forming words or the beginnings of words, her eyes flicker.

They go to the gown and back to the screen again. *Come on*, I'm thinking, *come on*.

And then the silence breaks apart into a million pieces and Kris Kristofferson and Willie are singing LOVING YOU WAS EASIER, our song back then, and I know we're on the dance floor at the reception, our first dance together as husband and wife, and Lily leans back on the couch more relaxed now while Kris is singing *coming close together with a feeling that I've never known before in my time* and I turn to the screen in time to see that second kiss which is just as public as the first one, with everyone watching us tinkling their knives against their wine glasses but this one's real, I remember this one all right, I can almost feel it, this one's just for us, just between us two people so much in love and there's nobody in the room at all but Sam and me.

I begin to sob into my hands. Can't stop it. Can't stop shaking. It's like every moment of the past two weeks is flooding through me all at once, pouring out of me, all these moments away from her and it isn't fair, it isn't right.

"Patrick? Patrick, what's wrong?"

And the voice is Sam's voice.

I feel like a jolt of electricity. It's almost the same as when I saw that snake. I've done it! I can't fucking believe it!

"Sam! jesus, Sam! Sam!"

I reach for her but she's up and off the couch so fast I don't even come close.

"I! Am! Not! SAM!" she screams, her face a twisted mask of frustration and anger and goddammit it's suddenly Lily again, Lily in full-bore tantrum mode as she bats my beer bottle off the table, tears away the fireplace screen and flings it across the room, sweeps my John D. McDonald books off the mantle and as I'm standing trying to grab hold of her and talk to her saying god knows what to try to calm her down as she throws the standing lamp so hard against the wall that the light bulb explodes sending Zoey into a panic so that she leaps off the couch landing hard on her arthritic legs, skitters across the floor and races out of the room.

Lily's screeching loud and high as she tears my framed Jack Kirby print of HULK COMICS #1 that I've had since I was seventeen off the wall and smashes it to the floor and she's barefoot and glass is everywhere—I never want to hear that screech again as long as I live, it's like an animal in pain—and then I hear another crash coming from the study.

"Stay there," I tell her. I'm thinking about the glass. "Don't move."

I know what I've got to do. My being here's no good. My being here's just making it worse. She's looking at me like she'd like to strangle me, tear my head from my shoulders so I back off and head for the study. At least I can see if my cat's all right. So that's what I do.

I hear the coffee table go over behind me.

In the study the first thing I see is my lightpad smashed beside the drafting table and my pages scattered all across the floor. There's Zoey huddled in the far corner of the room beneath the window. She must have made a leap for the high ground and failed. Glass crunches underfoot as I go to her, reach down. She cringes. But I persist.

"Hey, girl. It's all right. It's okay. It's all right."

It's not all right at all but in a moment or two she relents and lets me touch her, stroke her back, scratch her head. Her eyes soften.

I'm hearing nothing from the living room so I'm hoping the worst is over. I figure I'll give it a little more time just to be sure.

I crouch beside the drafting table to gather up my pages and the world suddenly tilts on me, nearly sends me down to all fours.

I'm staring at the pages.

I'm looking at Doctor Gypsum and Samantha.

Only I'm *not* looking at Doctor Gypsum and Samantha.

I'm looking at myself. Myself and Lily.

In every frame. I've drawn us exactly. Our faces, our bodies. Lily's and mine.

Battling the Abominations League. Stepping out of the rubble of an old building, wounded, taking shelter, healing. More battles, more wounds. Whirling through space. Diving deep into the safety of the sea.

I've been doing this every day for weeks now.

I stare at the pages and feel a weariness I've never known.

I gather them up and place them carefully on the table.

Then turn and leave the room.

LILY'S STANDING WHERE I LEFT HER. THE TABLE overturned beside her. The living room is a shambles. There's an acrid electric smell in the air.

She's naked. The wedding dress lies torn and crumbled at her feet. And she's cut herself. On the hem of her dress are three drops and one long bright smear of blood.

She's crying softly. Her shoulders trembling.

"Lily."

"I'm not Sam," she says.

Only gently this time. Almost, I think, with regret.

"I know," I tell her. "I know."

And then a moment later, "don't move. I'll come to you."

I cross the room and sweep her carefully up into my arms. Her face is still wet with tears against my cheek as I carry her into our bedroom. I lay her down on the bed and have a look at the cut on her foot. It's not too bad. I go to the bathroom for sterile pads and peroxide, bandages and bacitracin. I tend to the wound.

The night's warm. She makes no move for the covers.

I lie down beside her and look into her eyes and she looks into mine. I don't know what she sees there but she holds my gaze and doesn't turn away. I'm not sure what I see in her eyes either. I think of Sam and I think of Lily. But in a little while I reach over.

It's perhaps a blessing, this thing I have, and perhaps a curse. I've always thought blessing but now I'm not so sure.

I know exactly how to touch her.

I know how to touch.

END

Who's Lily?

IDON'T KNOW WHAT IN HELL IS GOING ON BUT I'M scared. My body is telling me something frightening and my body doesn't lie.

As soon as I'm awake I can feel the wetness inside me—Patrick last night—so I roll away from him still asleep beside me, and as I stand his semen starts to ooze and slide along the inside of my left thigh. It's just barely dawn. It's still dark inside the house but I'd know my way to the bathroom blind. I use some toilet paper on my leg and labia and then a warm wet facecloth for your basic whore's bath, thinking I really need to depilate or wax down there, wondering how I've let it go this long, and that's when I notice my legs.

My legs are unshaven.

I run the palms of my hands up and down over them and that's stubble all right. I'd say about two-or-three-weeks' growth of stubble.

What the hell?

I stare at my face in the mirror. My face looks the same. But something about my hair's wrong. I had it cut and styled just last week but you wouldn't know it now. It needs a good brushing and it might be my imagination but I could swear it's longer than it ought to be—longer than it was just last night.

I reach up into it to shake it out and stop midway.

There are light thin tufts of hair growing out of my armpits.

This is not possible.

What my eyes are reporting my brain can't process.

I feel something drop in the pit of my stomach and it isn't hunger pangs, it's nausea.

I need to talk to Patrick right away.

But in the hall I glance to my right, and what I see in the living room stops me in my tracks.

My first thought is that we've been vandalized while we were sleeping, but I doubt that even a morphine drip would allow us to sleep this soundly. I step down the hall but not too far. There's glass all over the living room floor, presumably from Patrick's shattered poster art lying there, among other things, and I'm barefoot.

That's when I realize the bottom of my foot's bandaged.

I don't remember doing that.

From where I stand I can see the overturned coffee table, the fireplace screen leaning over against the far wall by the television—mercifully intact—Patrick's mystery books scattered everywhere, a broken Corona bottle, our vintage '40s standing lamp lying in the middle of the floor, its bulb down to filaments and its painted glass shade in pieces. And beside it lies a pale white dress.

I inch a little closer, mindful of all the glass, just to make sure that I'm seeing what I think I'm seeing.

It's my wedding dress, veil and all, crumpled up and torn and stained with what looks like dried blood.

I'm a medical examiner. I see a good deal of dried blood. And even at this distance I'm pretty sure that's what it is.

Connection: foot to blood.

And while all this is spinning around in my head, while I'm trying to take in and make sense of all this violence to our lives and property not to mention what's happened to my body, I realize that I've missed something so incongruous as to be almost surreal. Lying propped up on the couch, looking undismayed and undisturbed, is a big stuffed dog I've never seen before, bright red, a life-sized baby doll, also unfamiliar to me, and Teddy, my very first stuffed animal.

If this is Oz, I want no goddamn part of it.

I run shuddering back into the bedroom, sit down beside Patrick on the bed, place my hand on his shoulder and shake him gently. I don't want to startle him but I need to have him awake. He needs to help me. I need to have someone explain all this.

"Patrick. Wake up."

He squints at me and runs his tongue over dry lips. "Lily?"

"*Lily?* Who's Lily?"

His eyes are open wide now. He rises up on one elbow.

"Sam? Is that you?"

"God, Patrick. Of course it's me. Look at me. I mean really *look* at me. What the hell's happening to me? And what's gone on out there in the living room?"

It seems at first he can't say anything. Then he shakes his head. He looks puzzled. Then he smiles. Then he laughs. Then he reaches for me and takes me in his arms, hugs me tight.

"Oh, jesus, Sam. You're back! Thank god!"

I feel like somebody's taken my head and shaken it, hard. I've never been so confused and so scared in my life. I never thought it was possible. Something is so terribly, terribly wrong here.

"What do you mean, back? Back from where?"

What I really want to ask him is, *have I gone crazy, Patrick? Is that it? Have I?*

I feel his body go rigid suddenly. It's as though he, too, is scared of something now. And then I feel him start to cry.

Patrick never cries.

It starts off slow but soon this is big, deep, whooping crying, like he can't even get his breath.

"Patrick, what...?"

For some reason just the sound of my voice seems to hurt him even more. He's bawling, unrestrained as a hungry baby. I hold him tight. I notice Zoey, our old arthritic tuxedo cat, watching us wide-eyed from the windowsill.

"What? What's the matter? What's going on?"

His body's wracked with sobs. He's scaring me further.

"Patrick, you have to talk to me!"

He won't.

We must be fifteen, twenty minutes like this. He clutches at me like he's drowning, like the sea is beating at him and I'm the only rock around. His fingers are digging into my shoulders. His tears are rolling down my collarbone, cooling over my breast. He wipes away snot with the back of his hand. He'll go quiet and then start all over again. I've never seen him like this. I don't say another thing. I hold him, rock him. I'm calmer somehow. Maybe it's simple exigencies—I need to take care of this first. I need to take care of him.

But he can't seem to stop. He's mumbling something into my shoulder, the same thing over and over.

Finally I make it out. *What've I done? What the hell have I done?*

"What do you mean? What are you talking about, Patrick?"

He shakes his head and clutches me even tighter. It's hurting.

"Patrick, who's Lily?"

Lily. On top of all the rest of this, is he talking about some fucking affair?

"I…you were…I couldn't…" That's all I can make out. The rest is incoherent, muttering, sobbing.

I'm thinking that no, it's not an affair. I know my husband. An affair he could admit to. This is something else.

I can hardly breathe. He's got to let go of me.

"Patrick. Patrick listen to me. You need to rest. You need to let go. I'll make us some coffee and we'll talk, okay? About…everything. Let me go, Patrick. Please. Let go."

He eases up slightly.

"Okay. Good," I tell him. "You're okay. You're going to be fine. Let me make us some coffee."

I have to use both hands to pry us apart.

His face is bathed in tears, his lips pulled away from his teeth as though frozen in some painful simulation of a smile. For a moment our eyes meet and I can't say what I see in his, whether it's pain or relief, joy or grief. It crosses my mind that he looks like some crazy religious penitent in the throes of ecstasy. And I wonder who's gone mad here, him or I or both of us.

I get up off the bed and go to the closet for my bathrobe. It's there all right, but not where I left it. It's pushed aside, as are my skirts and jackets for work, and for the first time I notice that there are clothes strewn all over the bedroom floor—my clothes—my red satin dress, my faux Hermes silk scarf, a pair of mismatched woolen knee-socks, my long white gloves.

Connection: clothes on the floor, my wedding dress destroyed in the living room.

I have no idea what this means but I think, *leave it go for later. Get the coffee. Patrick needs the coffee and probably so do you.* I slip on the bathrobe and knot it around my waist.

The coffeepot's in the sink and there are grounds in the bottom so I wash it out and fill it with water to the ten-mark, because this could be a multi-cup morning, and turn to the Krups machine on the counter and at first I don't register what I'm seeing. It's bright purple and has a clock and a dial and it's shaped sort of like an old-fashioned radio. Then I see the Easy-Bake logo.

Connection: Easy-Bake oven, stuffed toys on the sofa.

Is there a child here?

I think, the guest room. Coffee can wait.

The answer is yes. There is indeed a kid around here somewhere—or at least there has been.

It's a little girl.

How do I know?

Forget the oven. There's a beading set on the dresser and a half-made knotted multicolored quilt on the floor by the bed next to something called a Stablemate Animal Hospital. I see a small bandaged mule out front. On the other side of the bed near the door my entire collection of Barbies are outfitted in bikinis and lying on lounge chairs in front of a plastic pool and slide. There's a pink convertible waiting out front.

On the night-table next to the bed is a half-finished glass of milk.

Tossed on the unmade bed there's a pink pair of pajamas in a smiling-monkey pattern.

A little girl's been here recently all right, but where is she now? Not the living room, kitchen or either bedroom. Maybe the office.

I check the office. No.

Possibly outside.

I take a turn around the house. It's already unseasonably warm even at this early hour though the grass feels refreshingly cool and damp against my feet. It's the first remotely pleasant sensation I've felt all morning. I walk all the way out to the dock by the river and back again. I walk over to the old slide and swing set.

No little girl—though the slide is polished smooth, the rust all gone, the seats on the swings have been sanded down and I notice there's been some soldering work done on the chains and hangers. Patrick? It's got to be.

Enough of this, I think. I don't care what he's going through. I need to talk to Patrick.

I march into the bedroom. He's dead asleep.

I take his shoulder and shake him. There's no response.

"Patrick?"

I shake him again, a lot less gently this time.

"Patrick, wake up."

I shake him a third time. His eyes flash open and his arm flies up and smacks my hand away, bats it so hard it hurts.

"Go away!"

I stand there, stunned.

This is not my Patrick. My Patrick would never do this. My Patrick would never dismiss me like some huge annoyance and certainly he'd never hit me. The Patrick I know and love is the gentlest man I've ever met. After eight years of marriage he still wants to hold my hand in public or drape his arm over my shoulder or around my waist. He still wants that one last kiss before we sleep.

His eyes are closed again, his breathing regular. I watch him. Not for long but I watch him. And once again I can't believe what I'm seeing. Because already he's fled consciousness. He's not faking. He's sound asleep.

This isn't right. It's not normal.

There's something wrong with him. There's something wrong with both of us.

It's warm in the bedroom but I'm trembling. I very much need to calm down. I'm thinking that maybe that coffee might help after all, so I go back into the kitchen and spoon the French roast into the paper filter, pour the water, turn the machine on and wait.

Waiting's hard.

A shower would help too. I know it would. I should clean myself up inside.

And I definitely need to shave.

The sheer *fact* that I need to shave boggles the mind. Hair doesn't grow like this overnight.

Overnight. Good god. *What day's today?*

I could turn on the television to find out but the television's in the living room and there's all that glass.

The computer. That's in the study.

I sit down at our desk and boot it up and then I'm waiting again, for Microsoft to do its thing. I type in our password and wait for Windows. Finally there's our desktop. I run the cursor over to the lower right-hand corner and get the time and then the date.

It's 6:46. The date is May 29th.

It can't be.

Yesterday was Friday, May 11th. I worked all day at the Tulsa ME's office, mostly on a fat drunken Dutchman who'd slammed his car into a tree and a farmer who died of a heart attack in an enormous pile of turkey shit. I came home, and Patrick and I showered and fucked, had leftovers and wine for dinner and then we fucked again. And that last one was pretty wonderful.

May 11th to May 29th. How the hell can that be? Short of coma, how is that possible? If it were coma I'd have awakened in a hospital, not in my husband's bed.

I've lost eighteen days somehow. Two and a half weeks!

I'm glad I'm sitting down.

I can hear the buzzer from the Krups machine in the kitchen. The coffee's ready. But I don't want the coffee anymore. I feel like anything I put in my stomach would come right back up again. I need to know what's happened to me.

Doc Richardson. John. He'd know I think—if anybody would. He's been our doctor forever. He qualifies as a friend by now. And I've got to tell him about Patrick too.

It's much too early to call, but I can try him in an hour or so. Meantime I'll have that shower. I've been sweating. I stink.

On the way to bathroom I look in on Patrick again. I think he may be dreaming. He hasn't moved. His mouth is open slightly and his brow is knit and his eyes are restless beneath the lids.

He's hiding in sleep. How well he's hiding isn't clear.

The shower feels wonderful. Our water pressure's fine and I turn it on full blast, standing with my back to the shower-head so that the warm sting of it pounds away at my neck and shoulders and creates a sort of white noise in my head.

I don't have to listen to myself think anymore.

I wash and condition my hair. I soap my armpits and shave away those tufts of fur. I shave my legs carefully so as not to nick the skin. I take my time at both these things and then I just stand there a while in the spray. I'll deal with my pubic hair some other time—for now I just wash myself clean, inside and out.

It's only when the water begins to chill that I turn it off and towel dry. If I could, I'd stay in there all morning until my skin begins to prune and pucker.

On any normal day I'd blow-dry my hair, I'd moisturize, but this is not a normal day. Now I do want that coffee. After the shower, I think my stomach can handle it. I slip on my robe and pad out into kitchen.

The microwave tells me it's seven-thirty. I've been in there almost an hour. I sit at the kitchen table and sip the strong hot coffee, black with two sugars. There's no cream. He's not picked any up for me. Patrick takes his black.

Doc's an early bird. He's the kind of old country black-bag doctor you hardly ever see anymore. He opens at eight. So at eight o'clock sharp I'm on the telephone.

My hands are shaking again. I don't think it's the coffee.

Millie, his receptionist-slash-nurse, picks up right away.

"Hi, Millie, it's Sam. Is he in yet?

There's a strange hesitant pause on the other end.

"Sam? Why, it's so good to hear from you, dear. I'll put you right through."

Then it's Doc on the line. He sounds surprised and happy.

"Sam! Damn, girl, you had us worried!"

And hearing *his* voice I can't keep the sudden tears out of my own. Rational Samantha Burke is having a complete and total meltdown on the telephone.

"John, what's...I don't understand...what's happening here...I don't...I've...somehow I've lost days, weeks, I don't remember...and Patrick won't...he's... he just...our living room's destroyed, and my wedding dress...John? Who's Lily?"

There's a silence.

"Sam, Lily's *you*." he says.

And that's how I learn that for eighteen days, I've been a little girl.

HE ASKS ME TO CALM DOWN AND TRY TO BEGIN AT the beginning so I tell him about waking up and Patrick's strange, scary reaction and his sleeping and the trashed living room and the children's toys and all the rest and I try to go slow but it's hard, I know I'm skipping over things, but he listens patiently without interrupting and then he tells me about Patrick bringing me to his office and his interview with me and the subsequent results of the MRI, which were negative. He tells me that Lily appeared to be a smart, polite child of about five or six years old. He tells me that apparently I'd suffered from selective memory loss and age regression—he avoids the phrase *split personality*—that I knew my cat Zoey, for instance, but not my husband.

"I gave him the name of a psychoanalyst to call, Sam. I wanted you to see her right away. For some reason Patrick wanted to try to bring you back himself. I guess he did."

"Will I...good god, John, is this going to happen to me again?"

"I honestly don't know. Will *you* try the therapist?"

"Of course I will."

"Good. And from what you're telling me, so should Patrick. Tell him to give you her name and number. I'd see Patrick myself today but I've got a meeting in Oklahoma City at ten o'clock and I'll be gone all afternoon. I'm really glad you caught me. Can you bring him in tomorrow?"

"Yes. I'll see to it."

"Okay, nine o'clock. In the meantime, let him rest. He's had quite a shock. And you might try to get some yourself. Any valium in the house, anything like that?"

"I think so. I'll check."

"If you need some, call Millie. I'll leave a prescription for you."

"Thanks, John. Thank you."

"You're welcome, Sam. You try to relax now, and I'll see you in the morning."

I sit down with the dregs of my coffee and think this over. It's a hell of a lot to take in all at once like this but that's true of the entire morning. I need Patrick to fill me in on all the rest of it but Doc said to let him rest, so I will. The thing to do, I think, is to get busy.

I'm going to put our house in order.

In the bedroom Patrick's turned away toward the window and Zoey's curled up in the crook of his arm. I walk over and scratch her neck and the top of her head. She's purring.

I hang up the robe and slip on a pair of panties, jeans, a Jimi Hendrix tank top and my running shoes and I'm ready. I close the bedroom door behind me against the noise I'm about to make and haul the Electrolux out of the hall closet and the trash basket out of the kitchen.

Zoey's favorite stuffed toy is lying near the baseboard at the entrance to our living room. I pick it up and inspect it for glass. It's clean. It's escaped the general devastation.

Our cat has the strangest relationship to this thing. Every now and then we'll hear her yowling, this loud sad mournful sound coming out of her, and every single time the toy's on the floor or the bed or the couch where she's deposited it right in front of her.

The toy's a tuxedo, just like her. Patrick's theory is that she thinks it's family—a dead or lost brother or sister possibly. I tell him that's morbid. But with that sound she makes, he might be right.

I toss it out of the way down the hall toward the bedroom and plug in the vacuum. It roars to life.

For a while after that all I'm really conscious of is my battle against the glass, the tinkling of glass through the metal wand. When I get to Patrick's framed Incredible Hulk poster, the beer bottle and the painted shade I carefully pick up the larger pieces and put them in the trash basket. The smaller ones fly through the wand.

Is a wand called a wand because it's magic? There's the momentary urge to giggle. I wonder what Lily's laugh was like.

I set the coffee table, standing lamp and fireplace screen to rights and shake out my wedding dress. I inspect it for damages. There's dried blood on the train. There's a small tear from the end of the zipper down, about an inch long. The blood can be cleaned and the tear repaired but the veil is hopeless, torn to pieces.

And that's when it hits me. *I did* this. The shattered glass, the overturned furniture, the torn dress.

I did all of it.

A little girl inside me. But also me.

Once I've got the place straightened up and I'm satisfied that all the glass is swept away I set to deconstructing what Lily's done while I was away. The wedding dress goes in the hamper for cleaning and repairs.

Teddy goes back behind the glass doors in the hutch in our bedroom. Patrick's still sleeping the sleep of the dead, if not the innocent. In the guestroom— her room—I gather up the Barbies, thinking I've got to get rid of those swimsuits at some point and dress them in their proper clothes, and put them in the hutch beside Teddy where they belong.

The boxes for all the toys are in the guest room closet. I'm not surprised to find them there. Patrick's an inveterate pack-rat.

For some reason I want that Easy-Bake oven out of my kitchen right away.

I pull the box out of the pile and in the kitchen, pack the entire ridiculous bright-purple thing away along with all its pans and moulds and boxes. I trek it back to the guest room and shove it deep under the bed.

That's when, for the second time, I notice the half-empty glass of milk on the bedside table. A shaft of sunlight through the trees turns the film on the glass opaque.

I wonder how long it's been sitting there. Usually a kid will want a glass of milk right before bedtime.

But last night I slept in *our* bed with Patrick, not here.

Connection: and this one hits me like a brick, complete with all its implications, implications I know suddenly that I've been avoiding ever since my talk with Doc this morning—*I woke up in his bed, our bed, finally Sam again, with Patrick's semen sliding out of me.*

I was wrong. He *was* unfaithful to me. *He slept with Lily.*

An image scuttles through my mind like a spider in a web. I'm sitting in a dark movie theatre with my Uncle Bill, who I love beyond all logic for his crooked smile, his deep blue eyes and his curly red hair. I'm ten years old so logic's not important. Love is.

Uncle Bill's come to live with us in the spare room, and much later I find out why. He's been under my dad's supervision. My father has vouched for him with the local police, all of whom he knows, and most of whom are friends. Bill is a former postal worker who's been caught stealing money and checks out of the mail. My father has made a deal to hush it up. It's either live with dad or go up on federal charges. Bill has wisely chosen the former.

But now in that movie theatre—lunch at Bonvini's Pizzeria and a day at the Colony Theatre being Bill's present to me for my tenth birthday—his hand has come to rest my bare left knee. To this day I can't recall what the movie was, though I know that I very much wanted to see it at the time, because all I remember is the fear and embarrassment, the humiliation I felt as that hand moved under my skirt, up my leg, over my thigh and between my legs, stroking me.

About a year ago I performed an autopsy on a nine-year-old girl who had hung herself from a pipe in the basement of their home with her father's belt. Suicides among children under twelve are rare, but not unheard of. This little girl carried visible signs of vaginal bruising and internal tearing. Her father had been fucking her with both his penis and, as it turned out, a hairbrush.

Suicide among children is rare, but we all know that child abuse is not.

I remember my rage that day. It wasn't at all professional. I managed to hide the fact from my co-workers, but when I came home Patrick got the full brunt of it for what must have been an hour, and he agreed with me that there were people out there who were people in name only, who had only a cosmetic connection to the rest of the human race, who lived their lives without empathy or sense of justice.

And now I'm angry. Angry at myself for never telling on Uncle Bill all those years ago. Angry at

Patrick for betraying me in this strange foreign way, and betraying his words to me that day.

I feel a slow burn building.

I know what Patrick's hiding from. He's hiding from the fact that last night, he was fucking a child. And he knew it.

I go to the bedroom. The bed's empty. Patrick's gone.

He's not in the living room. He's in the kitchen. He's pouring himself a cup of coffee. He's pulled on a pair of boxers and when he hears me behind him he turns around. He looks like hell.

"What did you do last night, Patrick?"

He stops mid-pour.

"I know all about Lily. I talked to Doc. I know everything. So I'm asking you to tell me about it. *What did you do?*"

He finishes pouring and slips the mug into the microwave.

"Do you hear me?"

He won't look at me. He presses the keypads on the microwave and it begins its steady wind-tunnel hum.

"You know what this makes you, don't you?"

I almost don't hear his reply.

"You're my wife, Sam," he says.

"Yes. But I wasn't your wife last night, was I? I was some little girl. According to Doc, six or seven years old. So how many times, Patrick? How many times did you fuck me? Did you fuck me every night for eighteen days? Did I put up a struggle or did I just let you?"

"NO! ONCE! I swear to you, once, only last night! Only last night! Never before that. And that was after days of you walking around half-naked, asking me to help you wash your hair in the bathtub, clip together your bathing suit, and seeing you in that wedding dress again—I thought it was you for a moment, Sam! I did! And when I called your name, when I tried to touch you, you just went berserk, you screamed at me *I'm not Sam,* you trashed the room! And then a little later you seemed to forgive me and you were out of the dress, the dress was on the floor, you were naked, and there was glass everywhere, and so I picked you up and carried you…"

"And you couldn't help yourself, is that it?"

There's no way I can keep the acid out of my voice. I can see he looks exhausted, defeated. To me that reads *weak* and at that moment I hate him for it.

"Why didn't you get *me* help, Patrick?"

"I don't know. I just wanted…"

"*You just wanted.* You selfish bastard!"

The microwave timer goes off and to me its routine everyday beep is suddenly as huge as a siren screaming, it angers me by its very normality, when absolutely nothing is normal anymore, and before I know it I'm standing in front of him pounding at his chest and swinging for his face so that he has to fend me off like a boxer and I'm screaming at him, *you bully! you baby-fucker! you repulsive son of a bitch!* and I realize my claws are out too, I'm going for his face while he's yelling *no no no no!* and then suddenly I hear this other sound behind me riding high and stunning over all the sounds we're making, shutting them down as abruptly as you turn off water from a tap.

It's Zoey in the doorway, and her yowling is that familiar yowl we've heard so many times before, but there's more to it now, it's more complex, a kind of mournful savage screech, as though heartbreak and torment were one and the same, and as I turn to her I see why. She's got her toy in front of her as always, her tiny counterpart, her tuxedo, but she's tearing at it now, pulling it apart with claws and teeth and glaring at us as though daring us to stop her.

A cat can be a terror eye to eye when it seems as though she's lost control as Zoey is now and a chill rockets up through my spine and I know my feet are immobile as solid stone, that I couldn't budge them for a billion dollars.

But Patrick can move his.

"ZOEY!" he shouts and claps his hands. At the same time he moves on her, stomping hard, each footfall shaking the floorboards, and then for a moment there's a standoff, Zoey's eyes burning at him, glittering, and Patrick advancing until she suddenly drops the toy and turns and silently runs away.

Patrick stoops and picks it up. He cups it in his hand.

"She's had this for how many years, now?" he says.

His voice is quiet and very sad.

"We scared her," I tell him. "We never shout. We drove her mad."

He nods. The microwave beeps again.

This time it's only a beep, just an ordinary beep from an ordinary machine.

"Patrick? Give it to me."

He places it in my hand. I study it for a moment. I'm studying it but I'm also far away, months and maybe years away. For his part Patrick seems to know that. He's silent.

"I can fix this," I tell him. "I can fix this, Patrick."

I can.